Totally Bound Publishing books by Edward Kendrick:

Yin and Yang
The Hit Man Cometh

I0571311

THE HIT MAN COMETH

EDWARD KENDRICK

The Hit Man Cometh
ISBN # 978-1-78430-348-8
©Copyright Edward Kendrick 2014
Cover Art by Posh Gosh ©Copyright November 2014
Interior text design by Claire Siemaszkiewicz
Totally Bound Publishing

Published in 2014 by Totally Bound Publishing, Newland House, The Point, Weaver Road, Lincoln, LN6 3QN, United Kingdom.

THE HIT MAN COMETH

Dedication

For all my friends who didn't believe I could write
something like this.

Chapter One

"One step closer and you're a dead man." Bram kept his gun aimed squarely at Gavin's chest.

"I'm dead either way, so I have nothing to lose," Gavin retorted with a grim smile, placing one foot in front of the other.

"Why? Why are you forcing me to do this?"

"Better you than someone I don't know."

"It doesn't have to end this way."

Gavin smiled crookedly. "Got a better idea?"

"Yeah, team up with me."

"Marsdon would love that, considering he's the one who sent you after me."

"He doesn't have to know," Bram replied quietly.

"You'd turn on him?"

"Let's just say it's an option."

Gavin frowned pensively. "If I were someone else, would it be?"

Bram shrugged, not lowering the gun. "Probably not. I've worked for him before. You know that. I complete a contract."

Gavin glanced at his script before replying. "Four times by last count."

"Yep. I won't say they were righteous kills, but they at least had some logic behind them. Not"—Bram grinned wryly—"that it matters to me one way or the other."

"So what makes this different?" Gavin couldn't resist rolling his eyes at that line.

"Cut!" Chris Filmore, the director, called out. "Damn it, Gav, do you think you might act a little more suspicious? The two of you are supposed to be bitter enemies after what happened. Now he's suggesting you team up. That's not supposed to sit right with you."

"This whole damned play doesn't sit right with me," Gavin snarled, walking to the edge of the stage to stare down at Chris. "Who wrote this dreck?" He waved his script. "Like I don't know. The Tom Clancy wannabe you're trying to get into your bed."

"You read it before you auditioned. You knew what..."

Gavin held up his hand to stop him. "I read *something*. For damned sure it wasn't this. He changes it on a whim, and you let him."

"To make it more exciting," Chris replied defensively.

"Bull. This"—Gavin tossed the script at the director—"is so fucked up even a two-year-old would laugh at it." Jumping off the stage, he spat, "I quit. Sue me if you want to but I'm not letting my name be associated with something this bad. No way, no how." With that, he strode up the aisle of the auditorium, barely noticing the man who sat in the back row, before pushing his way through the doors to the lobby.

* * * *

Mick rapped one knuckle against his teeth as he watched the handsome, dark-haired man walk past him. *What an ass. No wonder someone wants him dead.* He chuckled under his breath as he got up to follow Gavin. *He has no idea how close to reality the play is, even if the author is, as he put it, a Clancy wannabe.*

Mick didn't know who had hired him for the job. The contract had come, as always, in a heavily encrypted email from his handler. The down payment, once he'd agreed to take the hit, had been wired to his offshore account. All he'd been told was where to find Mr. Gavin Wilde. Nothing about why. *It could be the result of some petty spat with a girlfriend – or ex-girlfriend. Perhaps another actor wanting the part. If it's the latter, maybe the hit will be called off now since Mr. Wilde just walked away.* He shrugged. *Somehow I doubt it's anything so minor. People don't pay my asking price unless someone has done them some serious hurt.*

He followed Gavin out of the theater into the afternoon heat, muttering, "This is Colorado, not Arizona. Why the hell does it feel like a sauna in early July?"

He chuckled when a pair of women walking by smiled, then one of them said, "That's what we were wondering too."

After wiping the sweat off his face, thankful that his blond hair was short now and not as long as it had been two weeks ago, he started after Gavin, keeping his distance. Not that the man would be aware of him, or anyone for that matter, Mick figured. *Not as fast and as angrily as he's striding along at the moment.*

When Gavin turned left onto a side street then went into a parking lot, Mick waited to be certain he had actually got into the dark red sports car Mick knew belonged to the actor. Then he hightailed it back to where he'd parked his motorcycle. He wasn't afraid of losing Gavin in the interim, as he'd put a tracking device on the car before going into the theater to check out his target.

Five minutes later, Mick, on his black Suzuki Bandit, hung back several car lengths behind Gavin as the actor veered onto Speer Boulevard. From the direction he was going in, Mick figured Gavin was heading home.

Mick knew he lived in a high-rise not too far from the Cherry Creek Mall, a very upscale shopping center in east Denver. He had cased the building soon after hitting town. Gavin was on the tenth floor in a north-facing condo, according to the information Mick had on him. The building's security was excellent, though nothing that Mick couldn't bypass with time or guile—whichever suited the moment. With some jobs, he might have been pissed that there were no tall buildings close enough to it that he could use one as a sniper base to take out his target, if things didn't work out right. Not with this one, however. That wasn't an option.

As soon as Gavin pulled into the parking area on the north side of the building, Mick found a place in the lot across the street. From where he sat, he could watch the balcony of Gavin's condo with the pair of high-powered binoculars he kept locked in his saddlebag along with the case holding his DRD tactical rifle, among other weapons. He was rewarded when the man walked onto the balcony a few minutes later, a glass in one hand, to lean against the railing.

Regretting your little temper tantrum? Mick figured, from the frown on Gavin's face, he might be doing just that.

Suddenly Gavin slammed his hand on the railing, spun around and went back inside. Less than five minutes later, Mick saw him leaving the building, heading to where he'd parked his car.

Now what's going on? Mick didn't have to wonder for long. He followed Gavin about ten blocks before the actor pulled into a parking spot just off Third on Clayton. Mick tailed him on his bike as Gavin walked to Second and entered The Cricket. Then he drove to the lot in front of a large health food store, locked the bike and strolled back to the bar. The place was busy, and loud. Mick eventually found a spot at the end of the bar where he could watch Gavin, who sat alone in a booth at the back of the room.

Not too much later, a young woman went over to Gavin, leaning on her hands on the table as she spoke to him. He smiled at her, nodded, and she slid in across from him. *One fact verified. His reputation as a womanizer holds true, from the look of it.*

Twenty minutes later, after drinking the beers a waitress had brought over for them, Gavin moved to sit beside the young woman. After a few more beers, the couple left. Mick followed them out into the cool air of midevening, then walked to where he'd parked his bike. When he checked the tracker, he realized the pair was headed back to Gavin's condo.

Or at least Gavin was, Mick soon found out. He got there just in time to see him park, exit the car, alone, then enter his building.

"Mucho strange," Mick muttered. He decided to give it a few minutes just in case the woman had driven over separately. When she didn't show, he kept an eye on the windows of Gavin's place, following the on and off of the lights as Gavin moved from what Mick knew — from the information he had — was the condo's living room on through to the bedroom. One by one, the lights popped on then off and soon darkness settled throughout the condo. "Pretty damned early to be going to bed," he commented. He was about to take off and figure out how to get into Mr. Wilde's place much later that night to do the job he'd been hired for. Then he saw a brief glow in the living room, as though Gavin had opened the front door, letting light in from the hallway.

Interesting. Is he heading to that woman's place, or somewhere else? Only one way to find out. He revved up his bike and waited.

* * * *

Gavin was just to the west of Golden, on Sixth, heading toward One Nineteen, when he spotted the motorcycle. It took him a moment to realize he'd seen it before, earlier in the day, as he'd driven home from the theater.

"Coincidence? Maybe," he murmured. "But I shouldn't count on it." He smiled dryly, checking the rear-view mirror again.

He continued well past Central City before taking a right onto a narrow two-lane road. A quarter of a mile later, just beyond a sharp curve, he pulled off to the side, the engine idling as he waited to see if he really was being followed. When the cyclist didn't appear, he figured it was just his overactive imagination at work. He continued on, until he came to a barely visible lane veering off to the left. A quick check as he pulled onto it let him know that no one had gone down it since his last visit — unless they'd walked in — as there were no fresh tire tracks in the dirt.

The lane wended its way through the tall pines for several miles before narrowing even more until the lower tree branches occasionally brushed the roof and sides of Gavin's car. Finally, he came to a small grassy clearing, with a cabin sitting in the center of it.

"Home sweet home away from home," he declared, following the last of the lane around to the rear of the cabin, parking, then retrieving his bag from the back seat.

He entered the cabin through the back door, walking down the short hallway into the living room and from there into the bedroom off to one side, using only the moonlight streaming in through the wide windows for illumination. Setting the bag down on the queen-size bed, he quickly unpacked. Not clothes — there were enough jeans and shirts hanging in the closet — but books and DVDs. Some of the books ended up on the nightstand. The rest of them, and the DVDs, he put on the shelves in the living room that held a small entertainment center. Then, still using just the moonlight, he walked into the kitchen. Taking a bottle of water from the fridge, he thought about fixing something to eat.

"Nah. I had enough calories in the beers tonight. Gotta keep my lean and hungry look." He chuckled at that thought and took a deep drink of water. "Not that it matters at the moment, I guess. What the hell possessed me to pull a snit fit just because of a lousy script? God only knows I've acted in worse plays in my day." As he talked to himself, he wandered back into the living room, stopping at one of the windows to stare out at the forest surrounding the cabin. For a second, he thought he saw something moving out there. *Stop being so paranoid. Probably just a mountain lion or a raccoon.* He was tempted to check it out, just to be certain. Then, with a shake of his head, he finished the water, tossing the bottle in the trashcan on his way to the bathroom.

A short time later, after a hot shower, he got into bed. Turning on the nightstand lamp, he picked up the book he was almost finished reading, contentedly immersing himself in the story until he fell asleep.

Chapter Two

Gavin woke instantly, every sense alert. He started to reach for the drawer in the nightstand.

"Move even a fraction of an inch more and you're a dead man."

Gavin looked at the man standing a few feet away, holding a rifle pointed at his chest, the moonlight putting him in silhouette. Feeling a strong sense of *déjà vu*, he retorted with a grim smile, "I'm dead either way, so I have nothing to lose."

The man chuckled but didn't lower the rifle. "That line is a bit like something a Clancy hero would say."

Gavin's eyes widened fractionally. "I take it you were there today. Ah. The man at the back of the house. Right?"

"Right."

"Hired killer, or did Chris send you to try to scare me into coming back?"

"Chris being the director?"

When Gavin nodded, the man chortled.

"I doubt he'd be willing, or even able, to pay me what that would cost."

"Hired then. By who?" Gavin asked.

"No clue."

Gavin thought about it. He could only think of one person who would want him dead, but he was the type who'd do it personally. Or he had been, four years ago. Looking hard at the man, he said, "May I at least know who my want-to-be assassin is so I can tell the police when they come to pick up your body?"

"Want-to-be?" The man chuckled. "I think I have the advantage here by a long shot, not to make a pun of it. But sure. I'm Mick." He eyed Gavin, grinning. "Do you really think you can move fast enough to stop me pulling the trigger?"

"Oh, I know I can."

Mick laughed. "Last I heard, The Flash was a comic book character, not a real human."

Rather than reply to that, Gavin asked, "Do you mind if I sit up? I promise not to make a try for my gun."

"Sure, be my guest. It makes you an even easier target."

Gavin did, slowly, being careful not to make any sudden moves. He started to swing his legs over the edge of the bed until Mick told him to stop.

"Why?" Gavin asked.

Mick replied, "Unless you're wearing shorts, or something, I prefer it if you keep the sheet over you. I don't want to be...shall we say...distracted."

Gavin slanted an eyebrow up. "A hired killer who lets something as mundane as a naked man distract him from his job?"

Mick shrugged. "Not usually, but it's been a long time and I'm looking at a prime Grade A hunk of male right now. Not that I'd actually do anything other than look."

"Do you realize how much you just revealed about yourself with those few words?"

"Yeah. It hardly matters, though. As much as I'm enjoying our little game of give and take, you're going to be dead in a matter of seconds. I have a plane to catch in a couple of hours and I didn't expect to be dragged into the mountains to finish the job."

"Why didn't you take me out in the city?"

"I was planning on it, until you suddenly took off and came up here. Your condo building may be secure, but trust me, someone dedicated to getting inside without anyone knowing can, and that's what I was going to do."

Gavin tensed as Mick lifted the rifle and he saw Mick's finger start to tighten on the trigger.

One second, Mick had Gavin in the rifle's sights as he started to pull the trigger. The next thing he knew, the rifle had been twisted out of his hands. Then a solid punch knocked him back on his ass.

"What the fuck?" he said in disbelief, rubbing his aching jaw.

"I did warn you," Gavin told him, kneeling beside Mick.

Mick stared at him for a long moment. Then he smiled slowly. "Next time I take a job, I'll make sure it's a human I'm going after."

Sitting back on his heels, Gavin asked without blinking an eye, "What makes you think I'm not one?"

"Oh, I don't know. Maybe because one minute we're discussing why I waited until you were up here to kill you. The next, you're showing me that's probably not happening unless I get a hell of a lot sneakier." He sat up, wincing again when he touched his jaw. "You pack a hell of a punch. Let me guess, fast, strong—a lion?"

"You're taking this all very calmly," Gavin replied. "And you're way off. Definitely not feline."

"Wolf?" Mick asked as he got to his feet.

"Nope."

"Gonna make me play twenty questions?" Mick held up one finger. "You're indigenous to what area of the country?"

Gavin chuckled as he stood as well. "All I want is an answer to my question then I'll tell you."

Mick obviously debated before replying. "All right. Part of the job is to make certain you're not only dead but that everyone thinks you just took off for parts unknown. You helped with the last bit by throwing your temper tantrum at the theater. All that was left for me to do was, as I said, get into your building and finish the job. Then you screwed things up."

"Sorry," Gavin said dryly. "So you followed me up here. How? I didn't see your cycle, if that was you behind me on the..."—he snapped his fingers—"You bugged my car."

"Yep. Something anybody in my profession does if he's worth his salt. Okay, I've answered your question so you owe me. What exactly are you?"

"A coyote." Gavin smiled. "Your turn again. Why weren't you surprised when you figured out I'm not totally human?"

"You're not the first shifter I've been sent after."

Gavin scowled at him. "You make it a practice to hire out to eliminate us?"

"Not really. About five years ago, I was after a man, well, a wolf actually, although I didn't know it at first. There was a high price on his head. Much higher than I figured was warranted, considering he was apparently a nonentity, so to speak." He chuckled. "The guy owned a tourist shop, for God's sake. Being nobody's fool, I decided to find out why someone wanted him dead. So I asked him."

"Why not ask the man who hired you?"

"I never have personal contact with any of the people who need my skills. I have a...friend...who knows people who know people. When he hears something, he gets in touch with me. It's all done by very highly encrypted email. It would take someone a hell of a lot better than anyone the government has working for them to break into it, thanks to my friend. Anyway, back to my story. I was somewhat leery of that particular job, figuring maybe it was a setup of some kind given the target. I decided to have a heart-to-heart with him. It was, shall we say, an eye-opener. He wasn't willing to die, so he showed me what he was then explained that he was the oldest son in his family and due to become the alpha when his father died, which was imminent. His brother, being a bit of a coward, had decided that rather than fight him for leadership, he'd just make certain he wasn't around. Permanently."

Gavin nodded. "Did you end up killing him anyway?"

Mick shook his head. "I took out the brother instead. That was the one and only time I've figured out who hired me, thanks to my target. And the only time I haven't completed a job I was contracted to do." He looked quizzically at Gavin. "I don't suppose you know who wants you dead?"

"I can think of one man, but he's definitely someone who would have come after me personally if he knew where to find me."

"You're hardly deep undercover, so to speak, considering what you do."

Gavin shrugged. "You might be surprised."

"Given how I live, probably not."

"So now what?" Gavin asked, strolling with seeming casualness to the bed. He sat, turning on the light as he did. With a slight smile, he pulled the sheet over his lap even though he was wearing a pair of sweat shorts.

"I do what I'm paid to." Mick picked up the rifle from where Gavin had dropped it before punching him. Much to his surprise, Gavin didn't try to stop him — yet.

"You don't give up, do you?"

"I'm stubborn that way." Mick raised the rifle, pointing it at Gavin. "Now, as I was saying, way back when—"

"I can take it from you again. But if I do, you'll just keep trying. Maybe not tonight, but sometime. Right?"

"Oh, yeah."

"So..." Gavin tapped his fingers together as he studied Mick. "How about we make a deal? You don't shoot me, and I let you fuck me. You said it's been a while since you—"

"Hold on just a damned minute," Mick said in disbelief. "You'd do that?"

"I don't have a death wish so..." Gavin spread his hands.

"But you're straight!"

With a laugh, Gavin replied, "That's what my agent would have everyone believe. I don't mind females on occasion. But my primary interest, if you would, is in males—especially dangerous ones. And, Mick, you are definitely very dangerous."

"Okay, what's the catch?"

"You mean other than bargaining for my life?"

"You're a shifter, damn it. You could take me in a heartbeat before I even pull the trigger," Mick said angrily. "You already proved that." The itch to squeeze off the shot that would end the job consumed him. But somewhere deep inside, he didn't want to. And he didn't know why.

"I did, and yes I could do it again. But to what end? Short of killing you, and that I won't do, because we'd be back to square one."

"Even to save your life?" Mick asked, lowering the rifle.

"Whoever hired you would just find someone else to come after me if I killed you. I'm not big on looking over my shoulder for the rest of my days."

"If what you said was true, aren't you doing that already?"

"Oh, it's true," Gavin replied adamantly.

"Who's after you?"

"What good would it do for me to tell you? You said you don't know who hired you, so even if I did, it wouldn't mean anything. And who knows? Perhaps I have more than one deadly enemy."

"Good point." Tired of holding the rifle — since he did not intend to use it, at least at the moment — Mick put it down on the dresser. Then he sat on the end of the bed.

"Why don't you know who hires you?" Gavin asked.

"For the same reason they don't know who they're hiring. No names, no chance of a double-cross."

"Your friend knows."

"Yeah. He's probably the only person in the world I trust on that level. We go back..." Suddenly Mick smiled. "You're good."

Gavin tilted his head in question.

"You have a way of making me talk about things I never do—with anyone—if that makes sense."

Chuckling, Gavin nodded. "It does. Part of being an actor is the ability to read and understand people. Part of being a coyote is... Well, a coyote isn't called 'the trickster' for nothing."

"Meaning the whole 'you'd let me fuck you' was just a trick to get me to let my guard down," Mick said, glaring at him angrily. Why he was angry, he wasn't sure. After all, Gavin had only been bargaining for his life.

"No, Mick, it wasn't," Gavin replied quietly.

Mick clenched his teeth to keep from saying what he wanted to. *Then prove it.*

Gavin cocked an eyebrow. "You're decidedly overdressed for me to do that."

"You fucker! You read minds too?"

"No." Gavin laughed. "As I said, I read faces and body language. Yours at that moment is very expressive." After moving the length of the bed until he was beside Mick, Gavin began unbuttoning the man's shirt.

Torn, Mick knew if he let this happen then in some strange way he was going against the code he had only broken once before. His own code that said when he took a job, he completed it. If he didn't let it happen, he might regret it for a very different reason. Against all common sense, he wanted Gavin. *How the hell can I want someone I don't even know? Okay, yeah, I want to screw him. It has been a long time since... But beyond that...* He shook his head. *This is insane.*

"Second thoughts?" Gavin asked dryly as he quickly divested Mick of his shirt. Before Mick could reply,

Gavin had him sprawled on his back and started undoing the closure on Mick's jeans.

"Lift," Gavin ordered.

Mick obeyed, watching with a mix of excitement and dismay when Gavin pulled the jeans down.

"Somehow, I expected you to be commando," Gavin commented while he finished undressing his now-willing victim.

Mick managed a weak chuckle. "Too damned uncomfortable."

"That it is," Gavin agreed before gripping Mick's hardening cock. When he took the pulsing head between his lips, Mick's moan seemed to echo off the bedroom walls. Gavin paused long enough to say, "Like that, do you?" He grinned wickedly, before continuing.

"Hell…yes! But…" Mick gasped when Gavin teased him with his tongue. "But… You should…"

Again Gavin stopped, this time to say, "Shifter here. I don't get sick, and so there's no need for a condom."

"Well… Damn. Who knew?"

Gavin grinned. "All shifters, and the men or women they have sex with. Now will you stop asking questions? At least for a little while."

Mick did, only because he was so aroused his mind couldn't form any more sane thoughts. Then, when he was certain that one more lick or suck would drive him over the edge, Gavin quit.

"I did promise you could fuck me," Gavin told him when Mick groaned in frustration. Opening the drawer of the nightstand, he took out a tube, handing it to Mick. Then he stripped off his shorts, got onto his knees and gripped the headboard with his hands.

Mick didn't need any more encouragement than that. Greasing two fingers, he pushed one through

Gavin's tight hole. After finding Gavin's gland, he stroked it and quickly had the man moaning deeply. With a second finger, he stretched Gavin until he sensed he was ready for the... He chuckled at his thought. *The* pièce de résistance. *That's a bit egotistical of me.*

It took only a moment to ready his hard dick. Then Mick pressed it to Gavin's entrance and thrust in. Mick saw Gavin's knuckles whiten as he gripped the headboard tightly, but the shifter never let out a sound that said Mick was hurting him. Mick knew he had, however, and eased back a bit before inching in slowly. Finally, fully engulfed in Gavin's tight channel, Mick let the fun begin as he rode Gavin fast and hard. Waves of ecstasy washed over him. He was only vaguely aware when Gavin's low groans of pain turned to gasps of pleasure. Then, with one final thrust, Mick came. As his orgasm consumed him, Gavin tightened around his throbbing cock. Seconds later, the shifter came as well.

When Mick regained some semblance of a working brain, he found himself lying prone against Gavin's back. Reluctantly he pulled out and slid onto the bed beside Gavin, saying sardonically, "Consider yourself safe, at least from me. You kept your end of the bargain. I'll keep mine."

Gavin smiled slightly. "And now you vanish into the moonlight? Or wherever hit men go when the job is finished?"

"Home," Mick replied. "Unfortunately that's not an option, because the job isn't finished, and I'm sure whoever it was who hired me will be aware of it all too soon."

"Damn." Gavin rolled onto his side, resting on one elbow as he looked at Mick. "I never really considered that."

"Why would you? It's not as if this is the norm for you."

"I beg to differ. Hiding is the norm. Okay, having someone like you coming after me isn't, but in theory, there are definite similarities." He lay back, staring at the ceiling. "I wish to hell I knew who sent you."

"I thought you did," Mick said, sitting cross-legged now to study him.

"I know who it might be, but as I said earlier this is not his style. If he knew where to find me, he'd have come himself."

"What did you do to piss this guy off enough that he wants you dead?"

"I stole…something from him."

"Money? Information? Drugs?"

"No. A woman, and not because I wanted her for my own. He'd kidnapped her, intending to sell her once he'd broken her." Gavin stared off into space, obviously remembering. "She was young and beautiful — and my daughter."

"Shit," Mick said softly.

"This man didn't know that at the time. He thought Mira was just another female I was interested in." Gavin smiled ruefully. "I suppose that doesn't speak well for how it appeared between the two of us. Being shifters, we age much more slowly than humans do once we reach our majority. So to all intents and purposes, we seemed to be close to the same age even though she was just twenty-two in actuality and had just stopped aging. Her mother was killed by hunters when she was ten, leaving me as her sole protector."

"Does this man know what you are?"

"Yes, because he's a supernatural being too. Unfortunately for me, he's a vampire, not a shifter."

Mick frowned. "Why didn't you kill him when you rescued your daughter?"

"Believe me, I wish I could have, but it's hard to kill something you can't see or sense unless they want you to. Even more so when your concentration centers on saving your child before she dies. He knew I was close by, he knew that I was a shifter and what I was capable of. So he did the one thing that would distract me until he could get away. He drained her until she was close to death. Another few drops and she would have become just a lovely corpse. My only choice was to transport her to one of our clinics and pray it would be in time to save her life."

"All right, I get all that, but surely he can't hold a grudge just because you essentially kidnapped her back from him."

"He lost face and a great deal of money. I think he could have handled the latter, but to lose face in front of the creature that had paid for her..." Gavin shook his head angrily "He swore he would find me and deal with me the way he had planned on doing with Mira."

"Is she at least safe now?"

Gavin sighed deeply. "As safe as one can be in their grave."

"Damn, Gav," Mick murmured.

"My one consolation is knowing she didn't become a vampire too."

"How long ago did this happen?" Mick asked, worrying his lower lip with his teeth.

"Four years ago."

Mick nodded. "Since then, you've managed to make a name for yourself, at least locally, as an actor. Is that really the smartest thing you could have done?"

"Considering Gavin Wilde isn't my given name, and I look very different from what I did then, it's not entirely stupid."

"Have you always acted?"

"In one way or another, yes. Not always on stage. I've had several careers in my lifetime. Some honest ones, most not so much."

"That brings up another point, since I'm being nosy—how old are you? You look like you're in your late twenties."

"I've been around for one hundred and eighty years."

Mick shot his eyebrows up and did a quick calculation. "You were born in eighteen thirty-four."

"Yes. Appalling, isn't it?" Gavin replied with a crooked grin.

"Does put an interesting twist on 'as old as the hills'." Mick started to reach out to Gavin then pulled back. "We should get dressed."

Gavin nodded. "We should. It's, umm, less distracting that way."

"Much," Mick agreed, getting off the bed.

He found his jeans and Gavin's shorts, tossing the latter to him. They dressed, more or less, as it was only in pants. But it helped.

"Who else might have hired me?" Mick asked, sitting again.

Gavin shrugged. "I suppose there are a few people in my lifetime who might be less than happy with me. Can't you call your friend to find out if he set this up?"

"He won't tell me any more than he'd tell the person who hired me who I am."

"Ah, right, you did say that, I guess

"So put your mind to it and try to figure out who we're dealing with."

"We?" Gavin looked at him in surprise.

Mick gave him a half-hearted grin. "Since it seems like I'm not going to kill you, I'd at least like to do something to keep anyone else from taking over the job. The only way to do that is to find out who wants you dead and why. Once we do, I'll deal with him, or her, if it turns out to be a female."

Gavin ran his hand through his hair in obvious frustration. "I have to think about it. I'm no saint. I've done some things in my life that I should regret."

"But you don't?"

"Probably no more than you regret killing people for money."

"Good point." Mick leaned back, looking at Gavin. "For starters, you can eliminate anyone you knew more than...say, forty years ago, if they're human. At this point, they'd figure you were too old to merit killing, or that you're already dead."

"You've never killed an older man or woman?"

"Well, yeah. Hate can run deep and last a long time in some people. So can greed, or the fear of blackmail, or a thousand other reasons someone wants a person eliminated."

"I will say this, I doubt whoever hired you is human. I haven't run a real con on one in years."

"You're a conman?" Mick chuckled. "I bet you were a good one. Hell, you conned me into not killing you."

"I was very good, in my day."

"Did you pull cons on shifters or other supernaturals? By the way, what other kinds are there—other than vampires?"

"That pretty much covers it. I've heard there are elves but that's only hearsay." Once again, Gavin seemed a bit bewildered at Mick's reactions. "I can understand you accepting what I am, since you dealt with a shifter once before, but you seem to be taking the idea that vampires—and perhaps other supes— exist as if it was an everyday occurrence."

"Hell, Gav, once I accepted that there are shifters it wasn't a big jump to figure there's other things out there. At least not to my way of thinking."

"True enough." Gavin glanced at the time, muttering, "No wonder I'm not firing on all four cylinders."

"My fault," Mick said, grinning slightly. "I should have dropped in earlier."

"Technically, you shouldn't have dropped in at all. Still, I suppose I'm glad you did. It made for an interesting night."

"My signal to leave?"

Gavin hesitated. "Look, it's late—or early—since the sun seems to be coming up. If you want to crash here instead of… Ah, never mind. You said you had a plane to catch."

"Had. I think it's a bit too late to make my flight at this point, if I really had one to make." Mick smiled wryly. "This was supposed to be a quick hit and run, not an all-night gab fest, so yeah, if you don't mind me using your couch, I'll take you up on your offer."

"No problem. The bathroom is…"

"Right by the back door. I passed it on my way in. By the way, you really should upgrade your security system."

"I only have it to scare off the occasional hiker that might happen on the place."

Mick snorted. "A lot of good it would do you if you're not here to deal with them." He started for the door then paused. "How many people know you even own this place?"

"That I know of? Three now. You, and two shifters I grew up with. Before you ask, I trust both of them implicitly."

"Hate to burst your bubble but at least one other person knows. Whoever you bought the place from."

"The land has belonged to my family since long before the pilgrims landed." Gavin yawned. "Look, if you don't mind, can we continue this conversation when we wake up?"

"Yeah, sure. Sorry. See you... Well, I won't say in the morning since it's nearly that now. Sometime this afternoon, probably."

Gavin nodded as he crawled into bed. "Oh, if you want sheets and a blanket, they're in the closet across from the bathroom."

"Thanks." Mick left the bedroom, stopping in the bathroom just long enough to piss and wash up a bit. Then, after getting linens from the closet, he settled on the sofa. As he fell asleep, he let his mind wander over the evening's occurrences. *What the hell have I gotten into, and more to the point, why?*

Chapter Three

Gavin awoke with a sense of *déjà vu*. Across the room, Mick stood looking at him. The only difference from last night was that he wasn't holding the rifle.

"What time is it?" Gavin inquired.

"A bit after three. In the afternoon."

Gavin chuckled. "I figured you didn't mean in the morning. There's too much sunlight." He sat up, stretching.

"Speaking of light, how the hell do you manage to have electricity?"

"Ever hear of propane generators? I have two, running in tandem."

"Okay. The fireplace in the living room is for heat?"

"Primarily."

"Next question…"

"Not until after I'm up, showered and dressed. Then we'll make an early dinner, given the hour, and talk." Gavin realized Mick had changed into different clothes than he had been wearing last night. "You have room on your bike to carry luggage?"

"Yep, since I pretty much live on it when I'm on a job like this one. Two saddlebags, one for clothes and necessities, the other for...other things."

"Like the rifle," Gavin said as he got up. "How do you manage that?"

Mick shook his head. "Go get ready then we'll talk. Your rules."

Several minutes later, Gavin joined Mick in the kitchen, somewhat surprised to find that he'd already started cooking. "Stew?"

"I'm not much of a cook, but I'm pretty good with this. I figured I owe you for what I put you through last night, so I'll play cook and you can watch and talk."

Chuckling, Gavin said, "You can't talk and cook at the same time?"

"Yeah, but I want to know how the hell you managed to build this place? It's not like there's a Home Depot right down the block where you can buy what you needed."

"Nope, but there is one in Denver, as well as appliance and furniture stores, and with the help of the two friends I mentioned, we managed to get what I needed up here."

"There's no way you could have trucked it up. Not on what barely passes for a road into here."

Gavin leaned against the counter, watching Mick toss the vegetables he'd cut up into the pot on the stove. "What do you know about shifters?"

"Not much other than that you can change between human and whatever animal you are."

"That's a start. We also have the power to teleport. So, to answer your question, we trucked the stuff as close as possible then teleported it the rest of the way. The cabin itself has been here since the early nineteen hundreds. Now that it's daylight, you can see that it's your basic log cabin that's been added on to over the years."

"Yeah, I noticed when I went to get my stuff from my bike. Well, not that it's that old but that it looks like something out of a history book. I figured you'd done that so it would blend in with the surroundings." He added the rest of the ingredients to the stew before asking, "Where does the water come from, and what about sewage?"

"The water's collected in a cistern, and there's a small septic tank for waste."

"So you're totally self-sufficient here?

"I am."

"Do you ever have strangers wandering onto the property?"

"Rarely, but as I said last night, it happens. That's why I have the security system, as rudimentary as it is, according to you."

"Very." Mick shook his head. "I'm a city dweller, born and bred. This is so out of my normal comfort range but it works, doesn't it?"

"Very well, actually. It gives me a place where I feel safe. Well"—Gavin smiled dryly—"where I did up until last night."

"Sorry to burst your bubble, but in the grand scheme of things, no one is safe anywhere if someone's dead set on finding them. And you, Gavin, were particularly stupid in that respect. Especially given the fact you could have teleported up here, then I would have lost track of you. Probably for good if you didn't go back to the city."

"Habit, I guess. I like having my car on tap, even up here. It saves making several trips to the grocery store when I run out of food."

"Yeah, well, from now on forget that inconvenience and leave it behind. The next guy who gets sent after you will undoubtedly do the same thing I did and put a tracker on it."

"Good point, I guess." Gavin got out bowls and silverware at that point so they could eat dinner when the stew was ready.

Later, as Mick dished out the stew, he said, "You told me only your two friends know about this place. Are you certain?"

"As much as I can be. I check as soon as I arrive, and so far I've never sensed that anyone has been around that I should worry about."

"If they're good at covering their tracks..."

"I usually do it in my coyote form. We have excellent eyesight and a very keen sense of smell."

"What if the person was also a shifter? Wouldn't you just figure it had been another coyote, or a wolf, or whatever who had been in the neighborhood?"

"No. Shifters have unique scents. A blend of both their human and animal sides." He shot Mick an irritated look as they sat to eat. "Are you trying to scare me?"

"Damned right." Mick picked up his spoon, waving it at Gavin. "I found you and I'm just a human. You said there were people, shifters, who might be annoyed enough with you that they wouldn't mind seeing you dead. One of them could be the person who hired me."

"That's what I don't get. If it was one of them, they could have tracked me down easily enough on their own."

"Without you being aware they were around?"

Gavin shook his head slowly. "No, I would have sensed them and taken appropriate steps to make certain they didn't kill me."

"Bingo. Does that include the vampire?"

"Good question. I'd say no. He's a totally different species with shielding abilities. Well, as I told you last night, when I was rescuing my daughter I didn't have any idea whether he was there too until it was too late. If I hadn't been able to teleport out of the room with her..." Gavin grimaced. "If I hadn't, you wouldn't have been looking for me because I'd probably be a sex slave or very dead—or at least undead."

Mick nodded, finally taking a bite of the stew. "Not too bad, if I do say so myself."

Gavin tried it and agreed. For the next few minutes their concentration stayed on eating, not talking.

Finally, Mick said, "Okay, this is off the top of my head, but what if it was the vampire who hired me?"

"I told you, he's the sort who would come after me in person."

"Maybe. Maybe not. He could be smart enough to know you'd be watching for him. I mean you are, aren't you? Isn't that why you changed your name and career and pretty much went undercover?"

"Yes," Gavin admitted. "Although I'd dearly love for him to show his face, I do know when I'm outmatched. But think about it, Mick. You had the information you needed to find me in the first place. I'm presuming that came from whoever hired you. If it was him, like I said, he would have come to Denver and dealt with me before I even knew he was around."

"Suppose that's not an option for some reason. It makes more sense that whoever wants you dead is someone who has known you recently."

"That's not what you said before. I think your words were, 'Hate can run deep and last a long time in some people'."

"And your vampire fits the bill quite nicely. Is there anyone else who would?"

Gavin frowned. "Not...that I can think of. I've made enemies but none who despised me *that* much." He shook his head. "They might want to see me beaten to a pulp, or other things of that nature. That happens when you run a successful con on someone and they lose a fair amount of money."

"Another thing. I'm sure you've changed your persona often in your lifetime, if for no other reason than that it would be hard to explain why you weren't aging."

"Much too often for that reason, and just to escape getting caught after I made off with a mark's money."

"Okay. So four years ago, you said the vampire— does he have a name?"

For some reason, Gavin found that amusing. "No, he just goes by 'the vampire'. Yes, he has a name. Clemente Valerio."

"Italian."

"Very much so. He was born there in the late eighteen hundreds and turned before the end of the century."

"How do you know that?"

"Trust me, once I found out who had kidnapped my daughter I did my research, as much as possible."

Resting his elbows on the table, after he'd pushed his bowl out of the way, Mick asked, "Do you know who he was planning on selling her to?"

"A friend of Magnus, his Sire."

"Just Magnus? No surname?"

"Just Magnus."

"I suppose he's pretty old too."

"According to rumors I was able to dig up about him, he was born late eleventh century AD in Norway."

Mick shook his head. "I'm beginning to feel like a baby compared to you and the people you hang out with."

"Not sure 'hang out with' is applicable in this case."

"You know what I mean. So, back to Clemente Valerio. You said he would have lost both money and face when you managed to rescue your daughter. What if this Magnus guy did something to him? Like maybe—what do you call it? I'm trying to remember what I've read in the myths. Put a compulsion on Clemente? So he couldn't come after you. After all, they for sure don't want us mere humans to know they exist."

Leaning back in his chair, Gavin thought about that. "I suppose it's possible, although I'm not human and I do know about them. But if Magnus were afraid Clemente would do something stupid… It's possible."

"Well, Clemente sounds like he's not the sharpest bulb in the pack if he kidnapped a shifter. So Magnus makes it impossible for Clemente to come after you on his own and Clemente does the next best thing. He finds out where you are. For him it might not be all that hard no matter what you think. Then he decides to hire a hit man to get rid of you once and for all."

"True, finding me would have been very difficult, but not impossible, I suppose, if he has the right connections."

"Exactly. He locates you, I am sent after you. Ta-dum, one dead shifter."

"Except I'm not, and if we're right, sooner or later he's going to know that."

"Sooner, since I won't be claiming the rest of the money he owes me."

"You could lie and say you finished the job."

"Umm, no. There was one proviso. He wants proof you're dead."

"Dare I ask what kind of proof?"

"I could say your head on a platter but it's not quite that bad. Just your right hand."

"Good God!"

"Yeah. Kind of hard to get it to him when it's still attached to your arm and I have the feeling you'd like it to remain there."

"Very much so. Do the people who hire you always want something that bloodthirsty?"

"Luckily, no. Most of my kills end up in police reports if not the news, letting whoever hired me know I completed the job. For the few that didn't, I was required to send pictures of the dead body."

Gavin got up at that point and began clearing the table. When Mick looked surprised at what seemed to be an abrupt end to their conversation, Gavin said, "Let's continue this in the living room, or better yet, out on the back stoop."

"Sure, why not? Hell, we can take a walk and talk. I could use the exercise." Mick patted his stomach. "I ate more than I probably should have but it was my first meal since, well, this time yesterday."

"I'm all for walking." Gavin smiled slyly. "Even running."

"Uh-huh. Have at it if you want but…" Then Mick obviously got what Gavin meant because he said, "You mean you'll shift and run."

"If you don't mind. It's been a while."

"Not a problem."

"Thank you." Gavin quickly washed the dishes and set them in the drainer to dry.

* * * *

When they got to the edge of the clearing surrounding the cabin, Mick saw there was a barely discernable path through the trees. When he asked, Gavin told him it led to a small pond about two miles away.

"Follow it, and I'll meet you there."

Mick wasn't certain he liked that idea. "What if I run into a bear or something?"

"You won't. Deer, probably, but nothing more dangerous than that. The predators know this is my territory and they won't bother you since you carry my scent."

"Hey, I showered when I got up."

Gavin laughed. "You've also been with me in the cabin since then and scents are transferable. You'll be fine."

"If you say so."

With that, Gavin shifted. His features elongated into a muzzle and his clothes vanished as he dropped to all fours, his arms becoming forelegs, fur covering his body, until a sleek, dark-gray coyote stood where Gavin had been seconds before. The fur on his lower body shaded to a tawny red with white fur on his throat and underbelly. The coyote looked up at Mick, a wicked glint in his eyes. If Mick hadn't known it was Gavin, he might have been afraid.

Instead, he just laughed, saying, "Go, have fun. And if I get lost, you'd better find me. A woodsman I'm not."

With a nod, and what almost looked like a grin, the coyote loped off into the trees.

Mick followed the trail, glad that it was still late afternoon with sunlight shining through the branches of the tall pines. He heard birds and occasional rustlings in the underbrush then the sound of the tree branches moving when a light breeze kicked up. Suddenly, several minutes into his walk, a deer appeared in front of him. It stood at attention, twitching its large ears, warily watching him. Given the fact that it had antlers, Mick knew it was a male and he prayed that it wouldn't attack. They faced off for a long moment then, with a twitch of its head, the deer bounded off into the trees.

Taking a deep breath, Mick continued. Then, he didn't know how much later, he saw the glint of sunshine reflecting off water. Relieved, even though he hadn't really thought he'd get lost, he crossed a small patch of grass to sit beside it and wait for Gavin to appear.

Something cold touched the back of his neck. Whirling around, he saw a coyote and hoped like hell it was Gavin. The coyote yipped, sounding more like a dog than some wild predator, then shifted, the fur vanishing as he returned to his human form, now fully clothed.

"Did I frighten you?" Gavin asked as he sat beside Mick. "I didn't mean to."

"Nah. Just startled me. How the hell did you do the whole instantly undressed, dressed again thing?"

"It's just part of being a shifter. If we had to take off our clothes first, we'd need to return to where we left them. Something that could be a real problem at times if we shifted to escape trouble.

"Makes sense to me, I guess. Did you have a good run?"

Gavin nodded, lying back with his hands behind his head. "I needed it."

"To get back in touch with your wild side?"

"Partly but also to run off the tension." He studied Mick for a moment. "Does what you do ever bother you?" he asked suddenly.

"If you mean do I feel guilty? Not too often. It's just a job and I figure if it wasn't me doing it, it would be someone else. Do the people I kill deserve to die? Apparently someone thinks so and who am I to argue?"

"Do I deserve to die?" Gavin asked tightly.

"Now that's a good question," Mick replied, wrapping his arms around his knees. "I didn't mean that the way it sounded. You're different. Not human—at least not totally human. Just like the first shifter I met. I suppose, because the circumstances are so different when it comes to him and you, it's hard to judge. The best way to describe it is that I'm dealing with something completely beyond rationale."

"So it's rational to kill another human, even when you don't know why they were marked for death, but not someone like me?"

"They're just targets."

"Not people."

"Not people I *know*," Mick replied. "Nor do I know anything about them other than the information given to me. They made an enemy for whatever reason. Did something bad enough that someone thinks they need to die because of it."

"How do you know that? I mean, I didn't do anything to Clemente—if he's the one who hired you—that was bad or evil. Neither did the other shifter whose brother wanted him dead so he could become the alpha."

"That's what I meant about you and him being different kinds of...cases. The rules, I guess you could say, that most people live by aren't the same when it comes to a supernatural. You all seem to have a predator–prey mentality. And before you get mad, you *are* predators. You kill to survive the way all wild animals do. Okay, so a vampire isn't an animal, but they are predators. Right?"

"True. Still, so are you."

"I guess. Yeah, I am. And a damned good one at that."

"What if you found out that someone you killed was, for lack of a better word, an innocent?"

"Meaning they didn't deserve to die?" Mick snorted. "Everyone dies, Gav. A lot of them don't deserve how they die. If you had cancer and it killed you, would you deserve that? No. But it would happen nonetheless. Does a kid who steps into the street and is hit by a car deserve it? Of course not. But it happens. I'm just the deadly disease or the speeding car."

"Only sometimes you aren't," Gavin replied quietly. "When you find out your target doesn't deserve to die... Well, to use your analogy, you veer the car away from the kid and he lives."

"That's happened only twice."

"Perhaps because you haven't met your victims face-to-face, except for me and him."

"Yeah, like I'm going to do that. With you two, it was just dumb luck that you turned out to be shifters."

"From what you told me, you made a point of talking to him first. Why not do that with everyone?"

"That hit seemed hinky," Mick muttered. "That's the only reason I talked to him."

"So maybe you should try that with all your targets."

"Not happening. I'm not stupid, Gav. I have information on them. It's pretty damned obvious there's a reason someone wants them dead. And it's not because they borrowed a lawnmower and didn't return it."

"How the hell did you get into this in the first place?"

"Easy enough—I needed money. I grew up poor, ran with kids just like me. Ones who were tired of being put down because they—we—weren't good enough"—he made finger quotes in the air—"to associate with the other kids in school, or church, or just those who lived a few streets away in a better neighborhood. We weren't a gang, not like you think of one, but we did things to make the guys who put us down wish they hadn't." Mick stared at the ground in front of him. "There's a feeling of power in knowing you can take on some bastard and show him who the boss really is. I liked that. I made a name for myself, of sorts. Then I met a man who needed what I had to offer." Mick raised his hands, balling them up into fists. "I was eighteen, a high school drop-out in a dead-end job. He was a"—Mick smiled dryly—"let's just say he was into distribution and needed me to protect his people. He paid well. Very well. Then, when I was twenty-four, he put me in touch with a guy he knew who needed a job done and done right."

"The one who's the middleman between you and your...clients?"

"Yeah. We hit it off. I did the job and, as they say, the rest is history."

"No guilt involved."

Mick shrugged. "Rarely. Hell, I couldn't do what I do if I did feel guilty afterward."

"I don't believe you."

Mick looked at him, shaking his head. "Why not?"

"The man I'm beginning to know has feelings and emotions."

"Doesn't everyone?"

"Okay, amend that. You have a sort of decency underneath the hard front you put out there. Well, I guess you put it out there. You did with me at first." Gavin chuckled softly. "Somehow, having you pointing a gun at me and watching you start to pull the trigger made me think you were less than pond scum. Since then, I've changed my mind. Like it or not, Mick, I see something in you that makes me think you could be a worthwhile human being."

"Don't try to go all Salvation Army on me, Gav. I'm far from that. Yeah, I don't want to see you dead, but only because I don't think it would be a righteous kill. Not if we're correct about who hired me."

"And killing other…" Gavin sighed. "Never mind. I think it's a losing battle at the moment. We should probably head back before it gets too dark. I might have superior eyesight but yours is just what any normal human has."

"Yeah. Poor me, just a normal human." Mick jumped to his feet. "Normal senses, low moral character, a real douchebag as far as you're concerned."

He stalked off toward the path, stopping when Gavin called out.

"You take that one you *will* regret it."

"Yeah? How come?"

"It doesn't go back to my place."

Mick frowned. "But it's the one I took getting here."

"Nope." Gavin came up beside him, pointing out a second path several yards away. "You were on that one. This one is just an animal trail. There's a family of deer in the area that made it coming to the pond on a regular basis."

"I saw the father, I think."

"Big ears like a mule?"

"I guess."

Gavin chuckled. "You are a city boy."

"Told you I was," Mick replied a bit petulantly as he headed toward the correct path.

"We'll change that, or at least expand your horizons."

Mick slanted an eyebrow. "Oh, yeah? What makes you think I'm sticking around long enough for that to happen?"

"You said you would. Well, sort of. And I don't think you'll take off until we find out who wants my hide pinned to a wall."

"No pun intended?" Mick asked with a bit of a smile.

"Well... Not much of one."

* * * *

They made it back to the cabin just as the last rays of sunlight disappeared behind the trees. Since the moon wasn't up yet, Gavin turned on the lamp beside the sofa then went to get bottles of water from the fridge.

"I do have some whiskey," he told Mick, "if you'd rather have that?"

"I don't drink."

"Really?"

"Yeah." Mick smiled wryly. "One bad habit I never picked up. That and smoking."

"I see. What about drugs?" Gavin asked, taking a seat at the other end of the sofa from Mick.

"Dabbled a bit. I didn't like losing control so I stopped. What about you?"

"An occasional beer."

"Then why have whiskey around?"

"One of my friends likes it when he drops in."

"Is that liable to happen any time soon?"

"Doubtful. He owns a business that keeps him tied up most of the year, and he has a family. He tends to come by only when he needs to get away and unwind for a couple of days."

"Would I be wrong in presuming when you said he drops in you mean he teleports?"

"As he puts it, he travels 'Air Bear'."

Mick nodded, rolling the bottle between his hands. Then, as if coming to a decision, he said, "Feel like screwing?"

"That was blunt," Gavin replied, somehow not surprised by the question.

"Figured why beat around the bush."

"What's the trade-off?"

Mick cocked his head, looking at Gavin. "Decent sex isn't enough, huh? Okay, I'll sweeten the pot. I will stick around so we can figure out how to draw whoever's after you out of the woodwork."

Gavin grinned. "I was teasing, but I won't turn down that offer."

"Damned conman," Mick grumbled but he smiled. "So, on your feet, because I'm for sure not fucking you on the sofa."

"I'm with you on that one," Gavin agreed, heading to the bedroom, flipping on the light before starting to strip. He was already half hard with the thought of what was coming. Then he turned to look at Mick. That finished the job. He saw a lean, lithe and muscular man who Gavin hadn't truly noticed in the pale moonlight the previous night. Mick's body seemed to radiate with energy—and that cock...

Gavin dropped to his knees to... *Well, I'm not sure worship is the right word but it works.* Gripping Mick's hips, Gavin laved his tongue from the base of Mick's cock to the already leaking tip before taking it into his mouth, sucking and licking then fully engulfing it. The groans he elicited from the man only served to encourage him.

Mick managed to gasp, "I can't...fuck you...if..."

Gavin released him, grinning. "No staying power?"

"I'll show you staying power," Mick muttered, pulling Gavin to his feet. "On the bed and on your knees—now!"

Anticipation of what was to come had Gavin instantly obeying Mick's order. He heard the drawer of the nightstand open and close, growling in frustration when Mick didn't immediately thrust a lubed finger into him.

"Patience," Mick said, smacking Gavin's ass.

Gavin's cock hardened even more, if that was possible.

Somehow, Mick picked up on that when Mick smacked him again a bit harder, murmuring, "You like pain. I sort of got that last night."

"Some," Gavin admitted. "Not addicted to it but..."

Mick brought his hand down hard on Gavin's butt then pushed two fingers through his tight entrance. When one touched his gland, Gavin almost came. Only Mick wrapping his fingers around the base of

Gavin's cock kept that from happening. Mick made quick work of readying him.

"Yes," Gavin gasped when Mick entered him hard and fast. The pain was intense. The pleasure that followed made it worth it. Gavin gripped the headboard hard enough that his fingers ached as the intensity of Mick's riding him increased, pain and ecstasy mingling to take Gavin to heights he'd never imagined possible. Too soon, his balls tightened and he exploded, almost passing out from the violence of his orgasm.

"Damn, Gav," Mick muttered once they'd both come down from their orgasmic highs. "Just... Damn."

For whatever reason, an inane line from some movie came to Gavin and he replied, "Was it as good for you as it was for me?"

"Fuck, yeah." Mick pulled out and moved to lie beside Gavin when he rolled onto his side. "Sex with you is...overwhelming." He brushed the sweat-soaked hair off Gavin's forehead in a gesture Gavin found very tender for such a tough man.

Gavin was tempted to kiss him then, but didn't, even though he very much wanted to. Mick wouldn't like it, because all this was just sex to him. Gavin could live with that—he thought. Instead, Gavin said, "We should clean up."

Mick laughed. "Yeah, you're probably sticky." He touched Gavin's chest. "Not probably. You are." Climbing off the bed, he held out his hand. "We can shower together and save water, a precious commodity around here I suspect."

Gavin let Mick pull him to his feet. "Pretty much so." He grinned. "We could always go back to the pond and take a midnight swim."

"If it wasn't so far away."

"Easily solved." Gavin slid his arm around Mick's waist and, seconds later, they stood at the edge of the pond.

"Holy shit!" Mick stared at Gavin with a mixture of shock and wonder.

Gavin chuckled. "Air Coyote."

"The only way to fly."

They did swim, though not for long, as the water was cold. Then Gavin transported them back to the cabin. When Mick started to take out the sheets and blanket he'd put back in the cupboard after sleeping on the sofa the previous night, Gavin said, "If you want a more comfortable bed, I'll share."

Mick hesitated. "Yeah, sure. But"—he tossed one sheet to Gavin—"we might want to use this. The one on the bed is probably…"

"Sticky or stiff by now," Gavin replied, catching it.

They made quick work of changing out the bottom sheet then fell into bed. They didn't hold each other, or even spoon together, which didn't surprise Gavin all that much. *Not his thing, I'm sure. Still, it would be nice.* He shelved the thought. *Be glad of the sex. Take it as given. God only knows I didn't really expect this to turn into more than that. Good sex then, once all this is over, 'Goodbye, it was nice knowing you' and we go back to our regularly scheduled lives.* He was surprised to find that the idea didn't sit as well with him as it should have.

Chapter Four

Mick awakened before Gavin. Deciding that staying in bed was not the brightest idea he'd ever had, because he knew how that might end, he got up and dressed. Then with nothing better to do, he went into the kitchen, contemplating what to make them for breakfast.

Better than thinking about what happened again last night.

He stared at the contents of the fridge.

Damned good sex is what happened. Nothing more. He's a nice guy. So what? As soon as we stop Clemente, or whoever's after him, it's over. I go on my way, he gets his life back.

He wasn't certain he liked that idea as much as he might have under different circumstances.

Quit. I'm all about working alone, with no...entanglements. It's the way it has to be. Fuck, I should have been faster. Should have pulled the trigger before...

Smiling wryly, he took out a half-full carton of eggs.

Before he offered to let me screw him. Should have said, 'Thanks but no thanks', done the job I'm being paid for and gone back to collect the rest of my money. But no. I let it happen, then I let him draw me into why someone wants him dead in the first place. Big mistake, Mick. Really big one.

He set the eggs on the counter, looked over when Gavin appeared and said, "Now for the big question."

"Scrambled or fried?" Gavin asked.

"Bacon or sausage."

"I have bacon?"

"Maybe?" Mick checked the fridge again. "Nope. Sausage and ham. So which one?"

"Sausage."

As they worked together to make breakfast, Mick realized Gavin was watching him while trying not to be obvious about it. Finally, he asked, "Am I doing this wrong?" as he stirred the eggs.

"Nope. Just wondered why you're still here. Sure, you said last night you'd stick around, but that was in the, umm…heat of the moment?"

"True, but that doesn't mean I was lying. I don't have many morals — I think we'll both agree on that — but I don't like the idea of someone with even less morals than me wanting you dead just because you showed up in time to save your daughter from becoming… I'm presuming a sex slave for that bastard's customer."

Gavin's expression darkened. "Exactly that, and she'd probably have been turned as well."

"Figured. You owe him for what happened, and I'm willing to help with the payback."

"Offer accepted. Again," Gavin replied with a tense smile.

"That means we have to be certain he's the one we should be after. Not that he doesn't deserve death from the sound of it but, if he isn't my client then we're no further along than we were when we started."

"Very true." Gavin paused long enough to put eggs and sausage on each of the plates he'd taken from the cupboard.

Mick dropped bread in the toaster before getting butter and water from the fridge. "You're surprisingly well stocked," he commented. "No coffee, though."

"I'll put it on the list since we need to go shopping."

"For?"

"Coffee, maybe chicken or fish so we're not eating stew again tonight."

"More lube." Mick smirked.

"If you say so."

"Trust me, I do." Mick retrieved the toast slices, buttered each one then sat to eat with Gavin.

When breakfast was over and the dishes washed, Gavin suggested they shop before doing anything else.

"Going to Air Coyote?" Mick asked hopefully.

"No. Suddenly showing up out of nowhere tends to scare the townsfolk. Besides it only takes about twenty minutes to get to the Country Store."

Mick chuckled at the idea of their showing up out of the blue, then suggested, "We can take my bike, if I empty out the saddlebags."

Gavin agreed, so Mick stashed his clothes in the bottom drawer of the dresser. Then he put the cases containing his guns safely away in a well-concealed space Gavin showed him under the floorboards in the bathroom. When Mick asked, Gavin said it came in handy for hiding the few valuables he had around the place if he expected to be gone for any length of time.

"Are you going to put the rifle in there too?" Gavin asked.

"Already is." Mick took one of the cases out again, opening it.

"Okay, I heard about those but never saw one broken down." Gavin looked it over. "Clever."

"And a lot safer than toting across my handlebars. Cops tend to frown on that."

"I'm sure."

After locking the door and arming the security, Gavin followed Mick out to his bike.

"Have you ever been on one of these before?" Mick asked once Gavin was seated behind him.

"Does an original Harley count? Back when they first came out."

"Whoa. Are you serious?"

"Very. It was…interesting and a long time ago, but I do remember I'm supposed to lean into the turn."

"Then you're good. I'll keep it down to twenty until we hit the main road. By then you should be okay with the feel of it." Mick handed Gavin the only helmet he had with him.

"What about you?" Gavin protested.

"I rarely use it anyway, unless I'm riding where they're required by law."

"Stupid," Gavin muttered.

Mick just laughed, waited until Gavin had donned the helmet, then took off.

* * * *

"Talk about small town," Mick said much later when they were back at the cabin. "I think I counted ten buildings that weren't houses. At least there was a gas station. Plus the diner, the Country Store, the clothing store and two auto repair places. Why two of those?"

Gavin shrugged as he finished putting away the few groceries he'd bought. "No clue."

"I'll make coffee." Mick opened the can, sniffing the aroma with a happy smile. "Then we talk."

"Okay."

When it was ready, Mick poured two cups of coffee, shaking his head when Gavin added cream from the container he'd just bought, and two heaping spoonfuls of sugar. "That's just gross. Can you even taste the coffee?"

"Yeah."

"Okay, what's going on?" Mick asked, frowning. "Why only one and two-word answers when you're usually so chatty."

"Just thinking."

"About?"

After taking a sip of his coffee, Gavin walked out to the back stoop and sat on the top step. Mick followed him, leaning against the railing with one foot on the bottom step.

"I was trying to figure out how to find Clemente," Gavin finally said. "We need to be back in the city. Back to my condo where I can do some research."

Mick nodded. "You found him once. Would he still be wherever that was?"

"No. It was at one of two clubs he owned. One that's now out of business." Gavin smiled grimly. "The fire made the nightly news. Burned the place to the ground." He looked up at Mick. "Before you ask, I made certain no one was inside."

"Nice of you. So that's out. Did he start up another one?"

"That's one of the things I need to find out."

"Where does he...? Never mind—if you knew where he lived he'd probably be toast by now."

"Definitely. When I was searching for him the first time, the clubs were the only addresses I found for him."

"Okay, that brings up something I should have asked before. How did you know he had your daughter?"

Gavin tapped his forehead. "Mira showed me, during one of her few lucid moments. I got an image of the place, mingled with the pain he was putting her through, trying to break her will. A cry for help."

Mick saw the agony from the memory in Gavin's expression and gripped his shoulder for a moment before pulling away again. "Whether he's the one who hired me or not, we're going to find the bastard and deal with him."

Gavin savored the comfort Mick offered him then missed it when he withdrew his hand. So Gavin replied more sharply than he might normally, "*If* we can. I've tried"—he spread his hands in exasperation—"with no luck."

"You've got help now. Between us, we'll track him down. You're right, though, we can't do it from here." He chuckled low. "And here we just stocked up on food."

Gavin smiled slightly. "We'll take it with us."

"Then let's get moving."

Mick repacked his things in the bike's saddlebags while Gavin put what he'd brought with him in the way of books into his travel bag. The fish, meat and other food items that wouldn't keep for long in the fridge went into a cooler that Gavin then put in the back seat of his car.

"One thing," Mick said before they took off. "Is there somewhere you can leave your car other than at your apartment building? No sense advertising that you're back."

"Good point. Yeah, there's a long-term parking garage about ten blocks away." He told Mick the address.

"Okay. I'll meet you there. Then all we have to do is figure out how to get you into the building without anyone knowing."

"All the tenants have access to the back door." Gavin snapped his fingers. "I'll be right back."

Now what? He found out a couple of minutes later when Gavin returned holding what looked like a ratty…something. He laughed when Gavin put on a wig that had obviously seen better days. "You know that makes you look like a homeless guy. Why the hell do you have it in the first place?"

Taking it off, Gavin replied, "I used it as part of a con I ran way back when. I got sort of attached to it, so when I came back here once the job was over, I brought it with me. It's been sitting on a shelf in my closet ever since, along with a few other mementos."

Mick shook his head. "Good thing the cops don't know about this place. I have a sneaking suspicion those mementos could tie you to several crimes."

"True. Not that it's a real worry. Most of them are from long before any police detective nowadays was even born." He got into his car, put the wig in the glove compartment then said, "Do you know how to get back to the city?"

Mick grinned. "I think I can figure it out once we get on the highway. I'll follow you until then."

* * * *

Mick pulled his bike up beside Gavin's car in the parking garage.

Gavin joined him, his bag slung over one shoulder and carrying the cooler. "Are you leaving the bike here?"

"I'd rather have it at your building, in case of emergencies. Is there a visitor's lot?"

"Yep. Along the east side of the building. Trouble is, you can't park there for more than twenty-four hours."

Mick tapped a knuckle against his lips then nodded. "That gives us time to figure something out. Hop on. I'll drop you off a block from the building." He grinned. "And don't forget to put on that weird wig. Go up to your place through the back. I'll go to the lobby and you can buzz me in. Fuck, you can just teleport in."

Gavin chuckled. "Why didn't I think of that? Probably because I got caught up in the whole covert operations thing we had going."

Their plan worked and a few minutes later, Mick looked around Gavin's condo with a great deal of interest. "Hell of a lot classier than the cabin."

There were hardwood floors and white walls in the living and dining room. Oak furniture, the sofa and chairs upholstered in dark beige and gold, took up the center of the main room. Mick liked the granite-tiled kitchen floor that matched the dark oak counters. There was a media room, a state-of-the-art computer sitting on an antique oak desk. The bedrooms—Mick wasn't certain he was happy that there were two of them—were carpeted, with king-sized beds and large, modern dressers. All the windows gave great views of the city, as did the balcony off the living room.

Gavin chuckled at his comment. "Costs a hell of a lot more too but it's worth it. Put your stuff in there" — he pointed to the guest bedroom — "then we'll fix a late lunch."

Mick placed his weapons cases on the shelf in the closet where he could get to them easily, then stashed his clothes in the dresser. His one good shirt and pair of slacks ended up on hangers in the closet, looking very lonely.

Gavin came in just as Mick had finished unpacking and leaned against the doorjamb. "I hope that's not all the clothes you own," he commented.

"Nope. I have a decent wardrobe. I just don't bring much of it with me when I'm on a job."

"Bring from where?"

Mick grinned. "From home, and no, I'm not telling you where that is. Like you and your cabin, my home is my safe place. My sanctuary."

"Understandable," Gavin replied with a small frown before changing the subject. "How do you feel about roast beef sandwiches and a salad?"

"Lead me to them."

"We have to make them first. Damn."

"That works."

They spent the next few minutes putting lunch together then took it into the media room to eat while Gavin booted up the computer and opened a file after entering the password for it.

"This is what little I've found out about Clemente so far, and it's probably pretty outdated since that was four years ago."

"Little is right," Mick agreed after pulling up a chair beside Gavin to read what information he had on the vampire. He snorted softly. "He wasn't very clever when it came to choosing aliases for his business ventures. Val Clemens and Larry Clement?"

"No one said he was smart. Just evil."

"Is this one" — Mick tapped the screen — "still up and running?"

"No, he closed it down right after the fire at the other club."

"That doesn't mean he hasn't opened more. They seem to be his thing if those two are any indication."

Gavin nodded, going on the Internet. "Let me do a search, although I doubt he'd have used those two names again."

"Probably not. Especially if he knew you were behind the fire."

"I'm sure he had to figure it was me." Gavin paused, opening a new document to list any variations he, then Mick, could come up with on Clemente's name.

"Try anagrams too," Mick suggested.

For Clemente there were four possibilities, if the vampire still owned clubs. There was one that might work anagramming Valerio, and another using his first and last name.

"And of course," Gavin pointed out, "this is assuming he's sticking to old habits. He did seem to have a thing for dance clubs."

They found two clubs, Element C and Malevolence Rite that were anagrams of Clemente and Clemente Valerio respectively.

"I'm not liking Element C," Mick said. "It's a supper club. And not in New Orleans like the others were. Malevolence Rite, however" — he tapped the screen again — "is right here in the heart of the Mile High City. Presuming we're not just grasping at straws."

"Which we are," Gavin pointed out.

A search online for Clemente Valerio per se, as well as the two aliases he'd used that Gavin knew about, brought up just what he'd expected — information he already had.

Mick leaned back, looking at Gavin. "How did you end up here when everything happened down in NOLA?"

"It's an area I know well, both the city and the mountains, since I owned a house here in Denver at one time. When I saw a casting call for the theater in a national trade paper, I visited a man I'd used before to get new ID and the references I needed."

"What are the chances this guy would have given that info to Clemente or someone he hired?"

Gavin shrugged. "It's possible, if the money was right. But first they'd have to find him."

"Throw enough money around in the right circles and anything is possible. Even if Clemente was going to come after you himself, he'd have done that, since he had to figure you would have gone into hiding. What about people you know, especially shifters? How many of them did you tell about what happened, and would any of them sell you out?"

"No!" Gavin replied adamantly. "I have two friends, the ones who know about the cabin. In my previous line of work, the fewer people I knew the better. Those two I would trust with my life."

Mick nodded, chuckling ruefully. "That's about where I stand, only you have one more than me."

"The joys of leading criminal lives. Few friends, if any, and for damned sure you don't let anyone get close to you unless you know they're not going to rat you out at some point in the future."

"And that's hard to know until it's too late — sometimes."

Gavin cocked his head in question. "Speaking from personal experience?"

"Yeah. Luckily I managed to avoid getting caught when he turned on me. Needless to say, he's now in an unmarked grave in the middle of nowhere. Some archeologist might dig him up in a few hundred years and wonder who he was and what happened to him."

"Remind me not to get on your bad side," Gavin said before turning back to the computer. "Malevolence Rite is owned by a holding company according to this. Fuck."

"Now what?"

"M. Angus Ltd. Rearrange the letters."

Mick thought for a second then grinned. "You have Magnus. Clemente's Sire."

"Bingo," Gavin said. "It could be his, or Clemente may just have used that name and own the holding company himself."

"How long has the club been open?" Mick asked, leaning over to see the monitor. "That doesn't tell us anything. It's been around for almost four years." Mick glanced at Gavin. "And it's a gay dance club. Did Clemente know?"

"That I'm gay? Unlikely. Remember, I told you he thought my Mira and I were a couple. Still..." He frowned deeply. "After he got his hands on her, who knows what information he might have been able to glean from her subconscious."

"Did she know about the cabin?"

"No. I kept anything having to do with that side of my life a secret from her. As far as she knew, growing up, I was just a salesman who traveled on occasion as part of the job. Before her death, we split our time between my house in New Orleans and the one I owned here."

"A good cover story. You might be right, though. He could have dug into her thoughts and found out more about you than you'd like, including your connection with Denver. So maybe he opens the club, using his Sire's holding company for backing, hoping you'll walk into it one day and he'll have you dead in his sights. Then he gets one of his people to take you out if he really is compelled not to do it himself."

"One explanation." Gavin began pacing. "I don't visit clubs, so he was out of luck in that respect. Maybe he got frustrated and started digging around, hoping to find me another way. As you said, he offers money to the right people and eventually gets the info he needs then hires you."

"He's sort of placing all his eggs in one basket, concentrating on Denver," Mick commented.

"Who says he is?" Gavin sat again and brought up M. Angus Ltd. "The company owns four other clubs scattered around the country, all catering to gays. All opened within the last few years."

"Clemente must really hate you. It costs *mucho dinero* to open one club, to say the least of five."

"He's rich. Besides which, if he knows what he's doing—and he does—the clubs make him more money than they cost to start up. Both the ones in New Orleans raked in the dough for him. Well,"— Gavin smiled maliciously—"until I burned the other one down."

"Okay, so maybe we have an idea where to find him, if we're right about Malevolence Rite. Getting to him is another thing, given what he is."

"Yeah." Gavin got up to pace again. "I could do the obvious and visit the place."

"If you did, could he compel you to stay or to go with him?"

"Maybe, maybe not. I'm both a shifter and older than him. Before you ask, Mira was so young he had no problem managing her despite her being a shifter." Gavin paused his pacing to look at Mick. "He could control you in a heartbeat since you're human."

"So could Magnus, since he's — what?"

"Over nine hundred."

Mick grimaced. "He'd probably have no problem at all controlling you."

"Unfortunately, very true. So let's hope he's not aiding and abetting Clemente."

"If he is, we're in deep shit."

Back to pacing again, Gavin seemed pensive. Then he nodded slowly, murmuring, "Torben."

"Who or what is a Torben?"

"He's a who. My bear friend. He's been around forever to hear him tell it, and he probably has been since grizzlies naturally have long lives to begin with. Add being a shifter on top of that with our regenerative powers that keep us seeming much younger than we are. In his case, we could have a very formidable ally, if he's willing to help us."

"Contact him," Mick ordered.

He shrugged when Gavin shot him a look of surprise.

"Please?"

"Better." Gavin shook his head as he took out his phone. He tapped the keyboard and almost immediately returned the phone to his pocket.

"Secret code?" Mick asked in amusement.

"Not really secret. I just told him I needed his help and where I am right now."

"But you didn't tell me which room," a deep, growly voice said from the doorway. A huge man, well over six feet tall and built like a linebacker, stood there. He eyed Mick before crossing to clap one massive hand on Gavin's shoulder. "So what's the problem and who's the human?"

"The problem will take a while to tell, and the human is Mick..." Gavin frowned. "You know, in all this time you never told me your last name."

"Whalen." Mick smiled, slightly. "You were taking a chance there, calling me a human. What if I didn't know about shifters?"

"His message to me was short and sweet, 'Need help, condo, he knows'. I did wonder who the 'he' was. Now I don't." Returning his attention to Gavin, Torben said, "Tell Daddy all, but first get me a drink, if you would."

"Let's take this into the living room then, where we can all get comfortable, because this is going to take a while," Gavin replied.

* * * *

"So let me make sure I have all the salient points," Torben said quite a while later after tossing back half of his third whiskey. "Mick here was hired to kill you by party unknown. Using somewhat dubious logic, Gav, you tell him everything there is to know about you because — even less logically — you think Clemente is the one who hired him because he can't come after you himself."

Gavin nodded. "That's it in a nutshell, although there was logic behind everything. Mick volunteered to help keep me alive..."

"Which goes against the grain from the get-go," Mick put in, chuckling.

Torben nodded, eyeing Gavin. "How did you con him into that? You left that out of the story."

"Let's just say it wasn't easy but I did."

Torben broke into a toothy grin, leaning over to Mick, who sat at the other end of the sofa, and said confidentially, "So you know he likes it rough."

"I heard that," Gavin said, unsuccessfully repressing a grin of his own, "and he knows. However, that's not important at the moment. Why do you think our settling on Clemente as Mick's client is illogical?"

"Okay, perhaps illogical was the wrong word. Suppose Clemente is setting you up to come to him somewhere he knows he'll be able to fight you on his own terms?"

"He could have done that without bringing Mick into the picture," Gavin protested.

"But what fun is that? My theory is that Clemente hires a hit man, knowing you'll easily stop him from killing you. But, it also alerts you that someone wants you dead. Now who would be the most likely candidate? Presume Clemente doesn't know anything about you other than what he was able to pull from Mira's mind."

"And that wouldn't be all that much other than that I'm a shifter with ties to New Orleans, which he knew, and Denver."

"Exactly," Torben replied. "Since she didn't know about your past...career, he wouldn't either. You badly screwed up his plans. He hates you for that and wants to take it out of your hide. Literally. But being a vampire, devious and evil, he doesn't just come for you. He wants you terrorized, jumping at every shadow, before he draws you into his net and destroys you."

Gavin looked at Mick questioningly. "Think he's right?"

"You're asking me?"

Gavin snorted. "You're the expert. You're the one who hunts people for a living."

Mick nodded slowly, considering what Torben had said. "Honest truth. It makes more sense than Clemente's Sire putting some sort of compulsion on him to keep him from coming after you, Gav. The only thing I see that bothers me is — why wait four years? Okay, two things. Why open all those clubs?"

"That last is easy. Owning and running clubs is what he does. It also makes it less obvious that Malevolence Rite could be a trap. He may hope I'll think it's just part of the chain. They all have 'Rite' in their name. Perhaps he did anagram his name for the one here, hoping I'm smart enough to figure it out, adding another layer of panic."

"I guess that makes sense, but four years before he starts putting his plan into motion?"

"Who knows, Mick," Torben said. "Possibly his Sire didn't compel him not to go after Gav. He just ordered him not to. A child is supposed to obey their Sire from what I understand. So Clemente hangs back, waiting until he thinks it's safe and that Magnus has forgotten all about it."

"Guess we won't find out until I walk into the trap, if that's what the club is," Gavin declared, looking at each man as if daring them to disagree or try to stop him.

"You are not doing that until we have a plan that will keep you safe and let us take Clemente out of the picture permanently," Mick stated in a tone of voice that brooked no argument.

Gavin tried not to take what Mick had said on a personal level. *He's just stating a fact. My getting caught, or worse, would be...counterproductive.* Still he couldn't help the small bit of hope that just perhaps Mick did...

Does he care about me as more than someone he's trying to protect? I doubt it.

Torben nodded. "It won't be easy."

"What is in life?" Mick muttered. "At least in our lives."

Chuckling, Torben replied, "My life is quite simple. Except, of course, when Gav decides to get into trouble."

"It wasn't my fault that mark happened to bring along a couple of bullyboys just in case," Gavin grumbled.

"Do tell," Mick said.

So Gavin did, with Torben's help. By the time they finished, Mick was laughing in disbelief.

"I'd say it's a good thing you got out of the business, Gav."

"Yeah, well... I blame it on... Never mind. I vote we take a break and get something to eat. I can hear Torben's stomach growling from here."

Mick eyed Gavin as they headed to the kitchen, muttering under his breath, "Put the blame on *Mame*, as the song says? Or in this case James?" He heard Torben chuckle and had the feeling he was on the right track. Not that he'd say anything. Gavin's past was just that—his past.

* * * *

Torben excused himself as soon as they had finished dinner, telling the others he had some family business to attend to. "My youngest daughter is going out on her first date and I intend to be there to put the fear of God into the young man."

"So now you're a god?" Gavin asked, laughing.

Torben flipped him off and promised to return first thing in the morning so they could come up with a final plan that wouldn't end up with all of them dead. Then he vanished.

"One trick I wish I knew," Mick commented as he and Gavin settled down in the living room with their coffees.

"It does have its advantages, as long as you don't rely on it too much. There are some out there who can keep us from teleporting and of course that usually happens at just the wrong moment."

"Don't you just think about where you want to be and you're there?"

"Ninety-eight percent of the time, yes. But if we run into someone who can interfere with our thoughts..." Gavin shrugged.

"Like a strong vampire?

"Exactly."

"So if things start to go south, Clemente could keep you from escaping?

"Him, probably not. I'm more worried about him bringing in an older vampire."

"Magnus."

Gavin shook his head. "I think we decided he's not a part of this. If he was, I'd have been dead four years ago, right after I saved... After I got Mira away from Clemente."

"You did the best you could," Mick said quietly.

"I've been telling myself that ever since it happened." Gavin rubbed his eyes. "In my head, I know that's probably the truth. My heart tells me otherwise. If I'd kept a better eye on her..." He sighed deeply.

"You couldn't have been with her twenty-four-seven, Gav. If Clemente saw her, and wanted her, he'd have found a way to get to her no matter what, being what he is. I think you know that."

Gavin replied, "I do."

Although it was apparent to Mick that he didn't totally believe it.

After taking a drink of coffee, Gavin said, "I need to…get my mind off everything for a while." Jumping to his feet, he headed to the media room, flipped on the TV then flopped down on the sofa, flicking through the channels.

"Find a comedy," Mick suggested, settling beside him.

Gavin paused his surfing at *The Bachelor*. "Does this one count?"

"No. That's a farce and a tragedy rolled up in a ball of stupidity."

Chuckling, Gavin continued searching. Every time he stopped on something, Mick made a caustic comment about the quality of the show.

Finally, Gavin handed him the remote, grumbling, "There has to be something on there you can put up with."

"Doubtful. Besides which, I don't think you need to be watching TV."

"Oh?" Gavin cocked one eyebrow in question.

"Nope. You need to be doing something that will help you totally unwind."

"And I suppose you know exactly what that is."

"I do. That is if you're willing to share your bed for a little while."

Gavin shook his head in amusement. "I think we've already established I am."

Mick pointed toward the bedroom. "Then move it."

"Is that an order?"

"Damned straight it is," Mick told him, noting the look of anticipation in Gavin's expression. "I want you naked by the time you get there."

Gavin leaped to his feet, tossing aside his clothes on the way to his bedroom.

Mick followed, snapping out before Gavin could get onto the bed, "Stand where you are, hands at your sides." When Gavin complied, Mick circled him slowly then came to a stop in front of him. He lowered his gaze to Gavin's rapidly hardening cock. "Do not move," he stated, leaving the room. He returned almost immediately, having retrieved a snap-on cock ring from his bag. *A toy I never got to use until now.* He hid a wry grimace as he put it around the base of Gavin's cock.

"Why the hell...?" Gavin started to ask.

Mick administered a sharp slap to his ass and said, "Did I tell you to talk?"

Gavin shook his head.

"I thought not." He pinched one of Gavin's nipples, then the other, smiling wickedly when the shifter's cock hardened even more. "On the bed, on your knees. Hands on the headboard."

Gavin complied instantly, gripping the top rail. Mick pulled two leather thongs from his pocket, quickly lashing Gavin's wrists to the rail. "It would have been cuffs, but I don't have any with me," he told him, chuckling low.

Then he stripped off his clothes, his thick cock springing to attention when it was finally free. "You want some of this?" he asked, stroking himself.

"Yes," Gavin whispered. That earned him two hard slaps on his ass and the admonishment that he wasn't to talk. When Gavin barely breathed out, "Yes, sir," Mick spanked him again.

"You're asking for it, aren't you?" He knew Gavin was, because that's what he needed. Especially right now, when his guilt over what had happened to Mira was once again eating at him.

Now I'm a psychologist? And why do I care? Why should his needing...absolution...? Why does it make this different from any other time? This is just sex. Right? Right. Mick smiled wryly while getting the lube he figured would be in the drawer of the nightstand. *Sex with a man who I might...* He shook his head adamantly in denial before crawling onto the bed. He slicked two fingers, pushing both of them through Gavin's tight entrance.

Gavin gasped then moaned when Mick began to stroke his gland. His noises intensified with each touch. Soon he rocked against Mick's teasing finger, begging, "Don't...stop."

His words were instantly rewarded by two fast, hard slaps to his ass and Mick pulling his fingers out.

"Maybe I should leave you like this," Mick said, running his fingers the length of Gavin's shaft. "It's a nice night for a long walk."

When Gavin tensed, shaking his head wildly, Mick chuckled.

"I won't," Mick stated. "I need you as much as you need me right now."

With that, Mick lubed his cock, pressed the weeping head to Gavin's entrance and thrust in, hard. He stopped immediately when Gavin cried out. *There's pain – then there's torture, which I am not going for.* Suddenly, Gavin pushed back, taking more of Mick into his passage. Mick got the message and despite or because of the deep groans from Gavin, he continued his assault on Gavin's tight channel.

While he thrust into Gavin, he wrapped one hand around Gavin's cock, pumping it in rhythm with his thrusts. Steeling himself against the rising pleasure, he vowed not to come until Gavin begged for release, wondering if Gavin would finally disobey him again and speak.

"Mick, please," Gavin finally implored. "Please…"

With those few words, just as his own orgasm began to consume him, Mick flicked open the cock ring and the two men came as one.

* * * *

"Feeling more relaxed?" Mick asked, gasping for breath as he pulled out and rolled off Gavin onto the bed.

"Much," Gavin replied. "Or I will be if you'll untie me."

"Hell. Sorry." Mick quickly did so, tossing the thongs on the nightstand.

Gavin rubbed his wrists. "That was damned intense…and fantastic."

"I do try to please," Mick retorted with a grin.

"You do it very well." Gavin was tempted to hug him, refraining only because he was certain Mick would pull away. Thus, he was more than shocked when Mick pulled him into a tight embrace. Without a word, not wanting to tempt fate, Gavin wrapped his arms around him in return. *Does he…? Is he beginning to care for me? Because I'm for damned sure growing fond of him. Nothing more — but if he walked away… Yeah, I'd miss the hell out of him and not just because of the sex.*

"Does it bother you that…?" Mick hesitated. "That I'm willing to hurt you? Even though I know it's what you want?"

"What I need, Mick," Gavin replied softly. "Especially tonight."

"I figured as much." Mick released Gavin, resting on one elbow to study him.

"What?" Gavin asked, feeling a bit like a specimen under a microscope.

Mick smiled. "Just…looking. Looking for clues to what makes a man like you accept me despite everything you know about me."

"I could be superficial and say it's because you offered to help me. That's *part* of it, of course. You know things I never will that will be useful when we face off against Clemente."

"Like how to kill without remorse," Mick said dryly.

"Yes. Although I don't think I'll feel any guilt when that happens. There's more to it, though. You're not a good man. Far from it. But you're a nice man when you try. I suspect, although I have no reason to think so, that when you kill, you do it quickly and cleanly. If I hadn't woken up that night I wouldn't have known I was dead. Unless there is something beyond this life. At which point, if there is, I might have started to regret the life I've led."

"I suspect there are very few people who wouldn't wish they'd done some things differently," Mick replied. "At least you won't have to find out…any of that, for a while yet."

"If everything goes the way we want with Clemente. If it doesn't…" Gavin shivered. "If it doesn't, we may all be in for a very long, undead life."

"Then we'll have to be doubly careful that we plan everything down to the last tiny detail."

Gavin laughed suddenly, much to his and Mick's surprise.

"This is a hell of a talk to have after some great sex," Gavin explained. "We're supposed to be basking in the afterglow."

Mick snorted, scrambling off the bed. "You bask if you want. I am going to take a shower and head to bed."

"This bed," Gavin said, patting it.

"Only if we change the sheets. Again."

"It can't be again," Gavin pointed out as he sat up. "This is our first time screwing in this bed."

"You know what I meant," Mick muttered, smacking Gavin's shoulder.

"Foreplay?" Gavin asked, smirking.

Mick just rolled his eyes before heading out of the room.

Gavin watched him go and smiled. *He is nice. Not good. Not in the least. But...nice in his own way. And not bad in bed. Not. At. All.*

Chapter Five

"Cons are what I do," Gavin said, looking at Torben and Mick who seated across the table from him.

"With greedy humans," Torben replied. "And you were good at it ninety times out of a hundred."

"Ninety-nine."

"Whatever," Torben smirked. "Be that as it may, Clemente is not human."

"Not only that, but he knows you," Mick pointed out, tapping his forehead. "You walk in there cold and he will pick up on who you are instantly."

"You're assuming he's there, and that he reads everyone who comes through the door."

"If the club's a trap..."

"And we think it is. I'll have to figure out how to shield my thoughts."

Mick frowned. "Wouldn't that sort of be like trying not to think 'elephant', if you get my meaning?"

"He's got a point, Gav." Torben rapped his fingers on the table. "How willing are you to trust a vampire if I vouch for her?"

Gavin and Mick both stared at him. "You know one?" Gavin asked.

Torben nodded. "She's an old friend. And when I say old, I mean *old* as in almost Ancient."

"Is that a status of some sort?" Mick asked. "It sounds like it."

"Vampires are like humans in that they designate their ages by titles, like Adolescent, Young Adult, etcetera. However, with them the time span is much greater. Old vamps are anywhere from a thousand to five thousand years old. Brynja is well over four thousand, although being female she refuses to reveal her exact age."

Mick thought for a moment. "So Clemente, who is over one hundred would be?"

"A Young Adult. And Magnus is Middle Aged."

"Making Magnus the greater threat by a long shot, if he has anything to do with this."

"True," Torben agreed. "*If* he does."

"Okay, so what if he doesn't? What if Clemente has brought in an old vampire to help him?"

Gavin smiled ironically. "Then I'd be dead. It's the same reason I agree that Magnus probably isn't involved. He could have dealt with me with no real problem." He paused, shaking his head. "No, I think this is all on Clemente's shoulders. He's playing a game with me because he can. In the end, he wants me so terrorized I'll grovel at his feet, begging him not to kill me, or worse yet, turn me. Then it's a guessing game which he would choose."

"All of this is a guessing game," Mick muttered.

"Indeed it is and that's why I suggest we bring Brynja into the picture if she's willing," Torben replied.

"To fight him if it comes down to it?" Mick asked.

"No," Torben said. "She wouldn't do that. She has made it a rule to stay out of vampire politics. However, she would, I think, be willing to shield Gav's thoughts when he goes to the club so that he can approach Clemente without Clemente being aware until it's too late. Then she'd step away and let nature take its course."

"Will she do that for me too? Because there's no way I'm letting Gav walk in there on his own."

"Only one way to find out." Torben took out his phone and made a call.

Mick could hear his end of the conversation. It consisted of a brief explanation of what the problem was, interspersed with long pauses.

Finally, he hung up. "She should be here within the hour."

"Air Vampire?" Mick asked with a small laugh.

"Something like that. While we're waiting, we need to find out a lot more about the club, starting with where it is and who it caters to."

"I know it's downtown," Gavin said, getting up. "It's a dance club and caters to gays." He beckoned the others to come with him, going into the media room. After booting up his computer, he went online and pulled up the Malevolence Rite website.

"If he is using it to trap you, Gav, don't believe much of any of the info on here, other than the address," Torben commented as he leaned over Gavin's shoulder to look at the home page.

"I disagree," Gavin replied. "What's here has to be the truth, because he wants customers. Trap or not, he's first and foremost a competent club owner who wants to make money from his projects."

"Then I'd be willing to bet there's more to it than what's showing up on the Home page. Click on the Gallery link."

When Gavin did, they all nodded in unison.

"It certainly lives up to the Malevolence name," Gavin said.

The few pictures of the place that were interspersed with those of the customers showed a large room dominant with black and the colors dark blue and red.

"A veritable horror Halloween setting," Mick muttered.

"Or," Gavin said thoughtfully, "a place that would interest guys in the Dom–sub culture. My bet is there's more going on than is shown here." He tapped the pictures on the screen.

Mick rubbed Gavin's shoulder. "That gives us a perfect reason to be checking out the joint."

"I am not wearing a collar," Gavin stated in reply.

"None of the people in those pictures are, so I think you're safe," Torben told him with a wide grin.

Mick rolled his eyes. "You know too much about his sex life."

"We're friends. What did you expect?"

"Perhaps a bit of civility, Tor?"

The soft, dulcet voice had all three men turning just as a beautiful woman came through the open window. She landed lightly then strolled over to give Torben a hug. Compared to Torben, she was tiny, maybe five feet tall at most, with blue eyes and a long golden-blonde braid that fell well below her waist. "Good afternoon, gentlemen. Tor, introduce me, please."

"Brynja, this is Gavin"—he nodded to him—"and the rather formidable man on his other side is Mick. He's…"

"Human," she interjected with a smile. "I won't hold it against him."

"Thank you," Mick said with a smile and a small bow.

She sat gracefully on the sofa along the wall opposite the computer desk, then she cast a jaundiced look at the large-screen TV. "Boys and their toys."

Mick chuckled, thinking she looked more like a little girl playing grownup than a four-thousand-year-old vampire.

"Looks can be deceiving, Mick," she said, smiling at his look of shock. "Yes, I can read your thoughts. I believe that's why you need my help — to keep your foe from being able to do the same."

"True, so I suppose I shouldn't have been surprised that you can."

"No, you shouldn't. Now, boys, what is the plan?"

"We have one?" Torben asked with a laugh.

"You had better have," Brynja replied sternly.

"The first step is me going to the club tonight to check it out," Mick said.

"Oh, yeah?" Gavin shook his head. "Not happening. You are not going there alone."

"He doesn't know me, Gav."

"But he can read you easily and as you pointed out, it's like not thinking of elephant."

Mick turned to look at her "So I bring Ms. — or is it Mrs. Brynja? — with me."

"Gay club, Mick, in case you forgot."

"Did you look at those pictures in their gallery? It's not exclusively male. Mostly, yeah, but there were a few females."

Gavin glanced at the monitor and sighed. "Okay, so you're right. You are still not going in there with just one small female..."

Mick and Brynja managed to hiss at the same time.

"Hired killer here," Mick snarled.

Immediately, she added, "Very experienced vampire who can take care of both of us."

"Guess you're outnumbered, Gav," Mick told him with a smirk.

"I don't like it."

"And I care why?" Mick gripped Gavin's shoulders, looking down at him. "The whole idea is to make him show himself but we have to know the territory we're dealing with first. Actually" — he glanced at Brynja — "having her along might be the best part of the plan if what I've heard about vampires is true. She can go to the ladies' room, come out invisible and explore the rest of the joint while I sit at the bar checking out the type of guys who frequent the place. We will want to fit in when we go there."

"One flaw in your brilliant plan. If he's checking people out, either in person or by security cameras, and you go in with her tonight, then come back tomorrow with me, it'll raise one big red flag," Gavin pointed out. "So, the three of us go tonight with Torben waiting outside in case we need backup."

"But..."

"He's right, Mick," Brynja said. "And so were you. I can go in invisible and I will. But" — she looked at each man in turn — "I believe your plan needs revising. After all, how will Clemente be able to go after Gavin if he isn't aware he's there?"

"I know what he looks like. I can..." Gavin frowned. "Do something to get him away somewhere private, perhaps to his office, then do what needs to be done."

"The moment he figures out who you are he'll try to enthrall you," Brynja said scathingly. "Don't think because you're a shifter and have been around for longer than he has that it would be impossible for him to do that. If Mick is with you, he'll do it to both of you unless" — she smiled wickedly — "I'm there too, to keep it from happening."

"Why don't we just set you on him?" Mick grumbled before he remembered what Torben had said about her unwillingness to get involved in vampire politics.

"Indeed," she said, obviously having read his mind again. "It's one thing to protect the two of you, but I will not fight him vampire to vampire. That goes against my personal code of ethics."

"Even though he's evil?"

"Mick, he could be the devil personified and I still wouldn't. Wars have been started for less and you do not want to know what happens when vampires go to war. It can be deadly to the humans within their territories. Research Roanoke Island if you don't believe me."

"All right. But you will do your best to be certain that Clemente doesn't read us until we're alone with him, and that we're not in his thrall when that happens?"

"That I will do."

* * * *

"We have a problem and we're not even inside," Gavin said quietly, looking at the short line of men in front of the club waiting for the doorman to check their IDs. They had driven over in Gavin's car after deciding it was better that they all come together, for the time being, leaving Mick's bike in the parking garage Gavin had been using to hide his car.

"Damn, I never thought about that," Mick replied with a worried frown.

Gavin resisted jumping when Brynja spoke.

"Fear not, my dears. He will look and not remember."

He knew she was there even though no one could see her, but having a disembodied voice coming out of nowhere was still disconcerting.

When their turn came, the young man at the door glanced at them and their IDs then waved them in. The main room of the club was just as they'd expected from the website, dark blue and red walls and black furnishings. A long bar took up most of the left side of the room. Banquettes with low tables in front of them surrounded the dance floor. Multi-colored spotlights lit the throng of dancers while the rest of the room remained in low light.

Mick and Gavin made their way to the bar. There was one vacant stool that Gavin quickly grabbed, beating out a slender blond man, who at first looked disgusted. Then, after raking his gaze over Gavin from head to toe, he said, "Can I at least squeeze in next to you? I'll even buy you a drink."

"I think not," Mick growled, possessively resting his hand on Gavin's shoulder.

With a muttered, "Oh, boy," the young man took off.

Gavin chuckled. "Now you know why I avoid clubs like the plague."

Mick grinned in response then flagged down the bartender, ordering beers for both of them.

"I thought you didn't drink," Gavin commented.

"I don't, but I can fake it when necessary." He leaned in to whisper, "Or Brynja can have it if she likes beer."

"I prefer a dry martini, but beer would do if I didn't think a floating glass would call attention to me," the vampire in question muttered in both their minds. "And close your mouths. You look like someone just goosed the two of you. Did you think I would talk aloud in here?"

"Well..." Gavin smiled wryly.

"Exactly."

Gavin took a drink, resisting a comment when, after he'd set his glass down, Mick surreptitiously switched their glasses. "Neat trick," he murmured.

"Whatever works." Mick managed to squeeze in sideways between Gavin and the man on the next stool then leaned against the bar while surveying the room. "If the way you described him still holds true, I'm not seeing him anywhere."

"Five ten or so, dark brown hair, an aquiline nose."

"Other than the nose, that would fit at least a third of the men out there. On the other hand, I seriously doubt that he would be dancing, or even sitting around watching."

Gavin looked up at the balcony along the wall opposite them. He didn't see Clemente among the men draped over it observing the dancers below them. "I don't suppose you can get a lock on him, Brynja, if he's in the building?"

"I haven't so far. We might want to explore the areas off to the side, and up and down the stairs."

It took Gavin a moment to realize that there were doors at the back of the room and that men were coming and going through them, usually in pairs. When he pointed it out to Mick, he got a nod in return.

"I saw that," Mick told him. "Private rooms or perhaps..."

"If he does cater to the Dom–sub element, there might be dungeons downstairs. Brynja suggested there's something down there."

Mick grinned wickedly. "Then, my young sub, let's go exploring."

"Young, my ass," Gavin muttered as he slid off the stool. He hated to admit it, but despite the reason they were there and the coming confrontation they'd be facing if they found Clemente, the idea of a dungeon had his cock twitching.

"That may be your thing," Brynja said acerbically, "but please don't envision it. It is not an image I want to be carrying with me."

"Sorry," Gavin murmured.

When Mick put his arm around Gavin's waist, asking what he was sorry for, Gavin told him.

Mick barked out a laugh before turning serious. "We have to act as if we know where we're going. I'd be willing to bet they don't let customers just wander around exploring."

"I'll lead the way," Brynja told both of them, "and make certain no one gives you any trouble."

"I think I love her," Mick whispered, getting chuckles from Gavin and, mentally, from Brynja.

When they reached the back of the club, they found that two of the doors, unsurprisingly, led to the restrooms. The third door opened onto a hallway. They saw there were stairs at one end leading up — at the other, a flight leading down.

"The offices are on the second floor. We might want to check them first," Brynja told both of them.

As they started toward the stairs, a man, who was obviously there to keep people from going up, stepped forward. A second later, he went back to leaning against the wall and the trio proceeded on their way.

When they got to the top of the stairs, they entered another hallway with four doors. Just as Gavin wondered which one, if any, belonged to Clemente's office, Brynja informed them, "Third door down, and he is in there with another vampire. One much older than him."

"Magnus, his Sire?" Gavin asked.

"Possibly. I can't read him. That means he is blocking and quite well, I'm afraid. I will do as I promised and not let them enthrall you. Beyond that, you are on your own."

"Thanks," Mick said dryly as he moved quickly down the corridor. "Stay behind me until I get the lay of the land, Gav."

Gavin didn't protest that he was quite capable of taking care of himself, given what he was. He understood that Mick was being Mick, the man who had to be in charge of any given situation that required the sort of skills he possessed. Out of bed, as well as in it. He smiled slightly then tensed when Mick opened the door, praying they'd both come out of this alive.

* * * *

"Mr. Wilde, I presume," a strikingly handsome man said, addressing Gavin. His long, black hair hung well below his shoulders. He pursed sensual lips and stared at him with piercing gray eyes.

"That would be me," Gavin replied, his gaze immediately going to the second man. It was Clemente, standing with his arms crossed, a feral smile on his thin lips.

Suddenly, Clemente frowned. "Why weren't we aware you were here, and...?" He scowled fiercely, his gaze flicking around the room as if expecting to land on someone hiding behind the desk or one of the chairs. "Who's helping you resist me?"

"What makes you think I need help?" Gavin replied with a calm he didn't feel. "I dealt with you once before and managed to snatch my daughter from under your nose."

"So this...human" — Clemente turned to stare at Mick — "is merely along for a pleasant evening of dancing and, dare I say, fucking in the dungeons?"

Rather than reply, and hoping Mick would remain quiet, Gavin turned his attention to the other man who he was certain had to be the vampire Magnus. "Your child has quite a mouth on him, Magnus," Gavin said with a disgusted shake of his head.

"Ah, you are aware of who I am."

Gavin nodded. "It was a guess, but a correct one, I take it. Are you here to help him, or just to watch while he tries to do his worst to me?"

Magnus smiled. "I am still debating that. He was ordered to stay away from you for the good of our kind. I would rather keep our presence secret, just as I'm certain you'd rather not let the world know shifters exist." As he spoke, Magnus seemed to be watching Mick more than Gavin. His smile deepened. "I surmise from the fact that he didn't show any shock or dismay at my statement, Mr. Wilde, that you are not averse to at least one human knowing about you. Or, I presume, about us." He gestured between himself and Clemente.

"Let's cut to the chase," Clemente growled, his fangs dropping and his nails elongating into claws. "I owe you one for making me lose face with the man who was going to buy your"—he leered—"quite lovely daughter."

Gavin stepped back a pace, readying himself while he said sarcastically, "How can a purveyor of flesh lose face with anyone? To know you is to know you are already the scum of the earth."

Clemente hissed angrily, only to stop suddenly, casting a horrified look at his Sire. "You can't mean that," he exclaimed, lowering his gaze to his clawed hands.

"Indeed I do. I told you what would happen should you pursue your insane plans." Magnus turned to Gavin. "Consider yourself lucky I happened to decide to visit him this evening, of all evenings."

A sudden thought hit Gavin. One he would handle later once the confrontation had ended. Instead, he replied quietly, "I feel very lucky. I really do hate—"

"Do not finish your statement. Shaming Clemente any more than he is would be the utmost in stupidity," Brynja cautioned him.

"I really do hate the idea," Gavin continued, changing what he was going to say, "that Clemente would be unwilling to forgive and forget our...misunderstanding." He couldn't help adding, "I'm certain you taught him better than that."

Magnus chuckled. "It seems I missed one lesson with him but I intend to rectify it soon enough." A pause followed then he nodded. "For now, however, as anticlimactic as it may seem, given that you came here intending to fight to the death with Clemente, you are free to leave. I promise you he will not bother you again."

From the look on Clemente's face, Gavin knew that didn't sit well with him.

Gavin nodded, telling the younger vampire, "I can't say this has been a pleasure, because it wasn't. If I had had my way, we would have ended this meeting with your death, and you know it. I have the feeling you might wish that's exactly what happened by the time your Sire has finished with you."

"I would have beaten you," Clemente replied sullenly. "After making you watch while I destroyed the human."

"I suppose we'll never know one way or the other, will we?" Then, with a small bow to Magnus, Gavin said, "Meeting you has been an unexpected pleasure, in more ways than one. I thank you for your timely arrival and hope that someday in the future we can meet again under less trying circumstances."

"It would be my pleasure," Magnus replied. "And if that happens, please bring both of your friends with you—the young human who was willing to die in your defense and the one waiting outside to come to your rescue if needed." He nodded, flittering his gaze around the room for a moment. "No, make that all three friends, the lady included, if you would. Now if you'll excuse us, Clemente and I have much to discuss."

"Again, many thanks," Gavin said. Turning, he led the way out of the office with Mick right behind him.

* * * *

"Magnus was right," Mick said a few moments later as they headed back down to the club. "That was more than anticlimactic. The thing of it is, how the hell did he find out we were coming here? Because for damned sure his showing up was no coincidence."

"Brynja?" Gavin looked around, wondering if she was still with them.

"Yes, dear boy?" she replied, becoming visible.

"Did you have anything to do with that?"

She shrugged delicately. "I might have had an acquaintance of mine put a bug in his ear while we were on our way here. Just as a...precautionary measure."

"You know, if he'd been willing to back up Clemente, we could have been in deep shit," Mick pointed out tightly.

"If..." Brynja nodded. "However, I know something of Magnus. He has a reputation for being a good vampire, in the grand scheme of things. I agree I was taking a chance, but I felt it was worth it. He is as aware as I am that while vampires and shifters hold no love for each other, a war between the two groups would be as devastating as one between vampire factions. When the word got out about a violent confrontation between Gavin and Clemente — and it would have — war might well have broken out no matter which one, Gavin or Clemente, prevailed."

"Not something I even considered when I decided to face him down," Gavin said quietly.

Brynja patted Gavin's arm. "Then it's a good thing Torben asked me to help you."

"Indeed it was," Gavin replied fervently.

"How did Magnus know you were actually in the room?" Mick asked. "I thought you said you just gave him a head's up that something was going down."

"I...lied?" she replied with an innocent look. "No, not really. All I did was warn him. However, he's clever enough to know I would also do my best to protect you, just in case, and that my being there was the most obvious way to do it."

"I almost pity Clemente at this point," Mick said. "Almost."

Brynja laughed. "I strongly suspect Magnus will teach him that disobedience has a heavy price."

"And if it doesn't take, Gavin will be back to wondering when the bastard will come after him again," Mick replied tightly.

"No. At that point, I hope Magnus will do what he should have when he first found out that Clemente was going against his orders concerning Gavin. He will wipe all memories of Gavin from Clemente's mind. Why he hadn't already is beyond me. I suppose he hated to admit to himself that, in that respect at least, he had lost control of his child. Something no Sire likes to acknowledge."

"No more than any parent does," Gavin said with a small smile.

"Indeed." Brynja stood on tiptoe to kiss Gavin's cheek. "And now I must take my leave. If you and Magnus do decide to get together sometime, let Torben know. I would love to join you. By the way, I've already told him we're finished here. He was glad to find out he didn't have to come in, guns blazing." She turned to Mick, kissing his cheek as well before saying, "Take care of Gavin."

Seconds later, she vanished.

"Take care of you?" Mick shook his head in bewilderment as he and Gavin went back downstairs to the main room of the club.

"Since I don't need taking care of, or protecting, now that this is over..." Gavin chuckled dryly. "I guess you're free to take off and return to your normal life, despite her orders to the contrary."

"I guess I am," Mick agreed. "Still..." He pointed to the crowded dance floor. "Do you...? Dance that is?"

Gavin looked at him in surprise. "I've been known to. Not at a club like this, and definitely not to music like this." He smiled sadly. "The last time was with my wife, not long before she was murdered by the hunters."

"I'm sorry," Mick said softly.

"As someone once said, it is what it is and in the past."

"Would you...? Do you want to gamble that we can dance and not make fools of ourselves?"

"Sure, why not?"

"I lead," Mick told him with a grin, pressing his hand to the small of Gavin's back to steer him toward their destination.

"And I should be surprised why?"

"I don't know?"

They entered the throng of dancers, finding space enough to move to the beat of the music. When Mick put his arms around Gavin, he could feel the man's tension. "It is over, Gav. You can unwind and start enjoying life again."

"I know." Gavin relaxed—marginally. Then he smiled. "I just have to figure out what I'm going to do."

Mick chuckled. "Start running cons again?"

"No. That's definitely not an option. It was very profitable but by the end, it stopped being fun and was just a job. A way to make money I really didn't need."

"You could go back to acting."

Gavin grimaced. "First I'd have to apologize to Chris."

When Mick cocked an eyebrow in question, Gavin reminded him that Chris was the director of the show.

"The one I stormed away from like a petulant child. At this point they've undoubtedly recast my role anyway."

"There are other theaters."

"True. And why are we discussing my future? We're supposed to be dancing."

"We can't dance and talk at the same time?" Then Mick realized they'd been standing in one spot and laughed. "Apparently not."

They did dance but not for long. Gavin still wasn't relaxing. Mick put it down to the fact that it was Clemente's club and Gavin couldn't forget that fact — and why they had come there. So he suggested they head out, to which Gavin readily agreed.

"Where to now?" Mick asked once they were outside the club.

Gavin shrugged. "Back to my place, I guess. Your stuff is there and you probably want to get packed up and —"

"Not at one in the morning." Mick started walking in the opposite direction from where they'd parked the car.

"Do you have a destination in mind?" Gavin asked, catching up with him.

"Not really."

Gavin frowned. "Just anywhere but back to condo. Right?"

"Yeah."

They walked a bit farther before Gavin asked, "Why?"

Mick smiled. "Is that an existential question? Like why do we exist? What is the meaning of life? What is my purpose?"

"No." Gavin came to a halt, waiting for Mick to realize that he had. It took the man a moment then he turned and came back to where Gavin stood looking at him in question.

"Why? Don't you want to go back with me?" Gavin said

"I didn't say that," Mick protested.

"Not in so many words," Gavin agreed.

"Look," Mick said, "we go back now and one of two things happen. I do pack up and leave, which I think is what you want, or I fuck you then I leave in the morning."

Gavin crossed his arms, looking at Mick. "Do you want to leave?"

"Given what I do, I doubt you'd consider my sticking around after tonight."

"Putting words in my mouth, Mick?"

"No, just stating a fact."

"It's not a fact if it's not true," Gavin replied quietly.

"You're shitting me!"

"That I'd like you to stick around? Nope. So you're not exactly a saint and what you do is definitely frowned on by ninety percent of the world, but..."

"Ninety-nine," Mick broke in with a small grin. "But who's counting?"

"Yeah, true. Anyway, what I'm trying to say is, if you want to stay, it's okay with me. I've got plenty of room. It would give you another safe place to live between jobs. If things got really hairy and a job went wrong, there's also the cabin."

"My jobs never go wrong," Mick muttered.

"Uh-huh. I can think of two you didn't complete."

"That's not what I meant and neither did you." Mick began pacing. "You're serious, aren't you?"

"Very."

"Why? I hate to throw cold water on your idea, but we barely know each other. So we like fucking. That's hardly the basis for deciding we'd make good roommates."

"We're two of a kind, Mick. Outsiders. You because of what you do. Me because of what I am."

"Still not a good reason to start sharing space together."

Gavin chuckled. "People have gotten married for worse reasons than that."

"Let's move," Mick said, the comment seemingly coming out of nowhere.

Gavin glanced around, spotted two police officers eyeing them and nodded. "No sense asking for trouble. We've had enough of that for one night."

They walked a block in silence before Mick said, "I guess there's no reason why we shouldn't at least try it. The worst that happens is we decide it's not working and I move on."

"And the best is that you have a second friend who will keep your secret no matter what."

Mick grinned. "And also likes a bit of down and dirty sex every now and then."

"That 'also' better not mean your other friend does and with you."

Mick broke out laughing. "Never asked him."

"Not that it would be any of my business if he did," Gavin said, "and that you'd taken advantage of it." *But for damned sure I don't like the idea. And that's stupid.*

"No it isn't your business," Mick said softly, "but like I told you way back when, until you came into the picture I'd been through a very long dry spell. Despite what you might think, I don't fuck every man I run into, as much as it might relieve the tension from a job."

Gavin studied Mick's face, looking for any tells that he was lying. Then he nodded. "I didn't think so but then, as you so succinctly pointed out, we barely know each other. Before you ask, neither do I."

"Honestly, I sort of figured that out for myself, Mr. I Don't Visit Clubs."

"That's not the only place to meet men," Gavin pointed out.

"No, but it's the best place if getting screwed is your thing." Mick shook his head. "Okay, time to drop this particular subject."

Gavin grinned. "Meaning when we get back to my place we're not going to do anything but sleep?"

Mick stretched and yawned. "Yep. It's late, we've had a rough night..."

Gavin gripped Mick's shoulder and instantly they appeared beside the car.

"Time to go home and see if you really mean that," Gavin said.

"You could have teleported us right to your place." Mick looked disappointed that Gavin hadn't.

"Then I'd have had to come back to get the car tomorrow, it would probably have had a dozen parking tickets, I'd have had to go down to the license bureau to pay them..."

"Okay, okay, I get the picture," Mick replied, laughing. As soon as Gavin unlocked the doors, Mick got in. "So how are you at breaking the speed limits?"

"Me, Officer? I wasn't speeding. Honest. So I was going a tad over the limit. It's late, I'm tired. I'm sorry?"

Mick snorted. "That won't wash, so take it easy. I might want your hot body but not at the risk of you getting stopped and me and a cop having to listen to that line of BS."

"*Might* want my body?" Gavin shot him a sour look before he started the car and pulled out into late night traffic. "Might?"

"Okay. I definitely want it. Better?"

"Much."

Chapter Six

With nothing on their schedules now, Mick and Gavin slept in the next morning — together — meaning no commuting between bedrooms for a wakeup bout of sex. Mick decided he could get used to the arrangement, presuming that it continued. As they'd said the previous night, they wouldn't know if sharing space was really going to work until they gave it a chance. *Sharing the bed — oh yeah — but are we really compatible enough to live together twenty-four-seven when I'm not off on a job?*

Thinking about work reminded Mick he had to check in with his friend. To do that, he needed his laptop with all its security bells and whistles. The laptop that at the moment was in the safe in Mick's home halfway across the country.

"Why the frown? Is something wrong?" Gavin asked, coming into the kitchen.

"I need to go back to my place. Meaning I have to book a flight," Mick replied, taking out his phone.

Gavin chuckled. "Need clean clothes? I do have a washer and dryer."

"I know, but yeah, more clothes would be a good idea and…" He wondered if mentioning he needed to find out if there was another job waiting for him was a good idea right now.

"And? Spit it out, Mick. If you're going to be living here, my first rule is no secrets. It's not safe for either of us if we're not open about things that could affect our lives on some level."

Mick nodded. "I need to get my laptop. Before you say I can use your computer, that's not an option."

"Meaning your laptop has more security on it than any of NSA's."

Chuckling, Mick replied, "Hopefully more, considering theirs were broken into."

"Okay, let's eat then go get what you need to bring back here."

It took Mick a second to figure out what Gavin meant. He grinned. "Air Coyote at my service?"

"Beats forking out a small fortune for plane fare, and it's door to door. Of course, you're going to have to let me know where we're going. Something you weren't willing to do a couple of days ago."

"Yeah, well at that point…" Mick shrugged.

"Believe me, I understand. You were just helping me out so it wasn't anything I needed to know." He smiled. "You wouldn't have known about the cabin if I'd teleported there instead of taking the car."

"If you had, this story would have had a whole different ending, and I'd be back to having just one friend."

"You never know. I could have stopped you here the same way I did at the cabin. Presuming you really could have gotten past the building's security and what I have on this place."

"Oh, I could have," Mick retorted. "Trust me on that one."

"Somehow, I believe you. That's beside the point, though. Let's eat, then you give me a visual of your place and we'll head out."

* * * *

"Not bad," Gavin commented when he and Mick landed in Mick's living room in what turned out to be a small, one-story house in a middle-class neighborhood.

"You expected something out of a bad forties gangster movie?" Mick asked with a grin.

"No. Well, maybe. For sure I didn't think of you living somewhere so...normal."

Mick laughed. "Why not? You think because I'm a professional killer I should be living in a dingy apartment with NRA posters on the walls and gun racks in every room?"

Gavin shot him a disgusted look. "Not even close but I guess I was figuring lots of leather and glass and steel furniture. A bachelor pad, so to speak."

"You don't have that and you're a bachelor. Most of this"—Mick swept out his arm—"is stuff I used to dream of having when I was a kid. Nice furniture like the stuff I saw on television, not the run-down second-hand stuff that was all my folks could afford. Yeah, it's not from the eighties, I have a bit more taste than that, but it's homey. Something I relish on my downtime."

"A place where you can get away from death," Gavin said quietly.

"Yeah, I guess." Mick crossed to the bedroom door with Gavin in tow. "Wait here, I'll just be a minute," Mick told him.

Gavin chuckled. "Will the bedroom destroy the homey illusion?"

"Nope. Hell, come on. I'm just being my usual secretive self when it comes to what I do."

Gavin found out what Mick meant when the man went to the wall opposite the bed. Mick moved the tall wardrobe that stood there to reveal an almost invisible door with a touchpad beside it. He tapped in a code, pressed his thumb to the bottom of the pad then opened the door, leading Gavin into what looked like a small office with steel cabinets, a metal desk and a safe.

"You sure you're not a CIA operative or a foreign agent?" Gavin asked dryly.

"Nope. Just real careful." At the safe, Mick took out the laptop he needed. "The rest of the stuff can stay here. I don't think you want me bringing more artillery to your place than I have already."

"It's up to you. Bring what you need."

Mick thought for a moment then shook his head. "I'm good for now."

After they returned to the bedroom, Mick got out a carry bag, filling it with slacks and shirts, as well as two pairs of jeans and T-shirts and more underwear. "That should do it," he told Gavin, putting the laptop in as well before zipping the bag closed.

Then Gavin teleported both of them back to his place.

* * * *

"Okay, you showed me yours, now I'll show you mine," Gavin said after Mick had unpacked. He was well aware that Mick would make some ribald comment in reply and he was right. He laughed then beckoned Mick to follow him. They ended up by the sliding doors in the living room that opened onto the balcony. Gavin moved a picture on the short wall perpendicular to them to reveal a touchpad. "Not as fancy as yours, I'm afraid. No thumbprint needed. But it does the job." He punched in a code and the wall swung inward.

"Panic room?" Mick asked, looking around.

"Yep. There's one in every unit but mine has a few modifications that don't show up on the floor plans." Moving a set of shelves holding non-perishable foods revealed a second, much smaller room. Like Mick's, it had steel cabinets on one wall, a table against the shorter end wall and a small safe.

"Okay." Mick blew out a long breath. "Why?"

"Why do I have this? I collect rare books. The cabinets are specially constructed to keep them safe from dust and insects. They're humidity and temperature controlled as well."

"How rare?"

"I have a copy of Twain's *The Adventures of Tom Sawyer* valued at ninety-two thousand, and a first edition of *The Wizard of Oz* that would sell for a minimum of one million."

Mick looked as if he'd been poleaxed. "You have got to be kidding me. How the hell...? I mean... Damn, Gav, how rich are you?"

"I'm not hurting but I'm not rolling in money either. You have to remember I've been around for a long time. I bought both those books soon after they were published. The same with some of the others that, in today's market, would bring in anywhere from twenty to forty thousand each if I were to sell them."

Mick managed a small chuckle. "So you're cash poor but assets rich."

"Not quite cash poor. But back to why I showed you all this in the first place. If you want to put your guns and what have you in here, be my guest."

"You're being awfully trusting, Gav," Mick replied. "Why?"

Gavin smiled. "Is that the watchword for the day— why?"

"Seems like it but that's not an answer."

Gavin didn't give him one until they were back in the living room. "You took a chance, showing me where you live and what's there. I'm just returning the favor."

"Thank you," Mick replied sincerely. "May I ask what's in the safe?"

"Provenance papers for the books proving who they were bought from originally and sold to afterwards. Of course, that was always me, in my various guises, but they are legit despite that. Also, several IDs." Gavin chuckled. "Those aren't so legit but so far no one's called me on that, even at the banks I use."

"Banks? Keeping your money spread out?"

"Don't you?"

"I use two banks for when I need ready cash, but most of my money is in an offshore account."

"Probably safer for you."

"Definitely. If it's good enough for some of our worthy—and I use the term loosely—politicians, it's good enough for me."

Gavin laughed at that. Then, after a long moment's thought and a nod of his head, he gave Mick the code to enter the panic room. "If I'm going to trust you, I'm going all the way with it."

Mick dipped his head in acknowledgment. "I'd do the same but our thumbprints don't match."

"That's okay. I doubt I'm going to need a full arsenal of guns and other weapons. They're not my thing."

"You've got your own weapons, built in, when you shift."

"Exactly. Close up I can definitely hold my own," Gavin agreed.

"Could you have with Clemente? He had a hell of a set of claws."

"Presuming he didn't go invisible, yeah, probably. Even if he did, I could smell where he was, and hear him move. I'd still have been at a disadvantage but..." Gavin shrugged. "Hopefully I'll never have to fight him now — or any other vampire."

"I'm with you on that one," Mick said adamantly. "I'll stick to humans."

"Who you don't fight," Gavin pointed out dryly.

"Not if I can help it. Speaking of which, I'd better check in."

"On your better-than-NSA-grade laptop," Gavin said with a grin.

"That would be the one. Mind if I set up in the media room after I put my cases in the panic room?"

"Not at all. You do that. I'll check in with the theater and see if I'm now officially *persona non grata*."

* * * *

As it turned out, Gavin wasn't *persona non grata* at the theater. In fact, when he called to talk to Chris, the director of the show Gavin had walked out on, the man practically begged him to come back.

"You were right," Chris admitted, "the script sucked. After due consideration, we decided, rather than ask for a complete rewrite, we'd do a different play instead, by another writer in the workshop. I know the scheduling is tight but if you're willing, I'll email you the script ASAP because I think you'd be perfect for the lead."

"As long as it's not another spy thriller knockoff," Gavin told him, chuckling.

"Far from it. It's a romantic comedy."

"Send it then. If I like it... When are tryouts?"

"They were yesterday." Chris sighed. "We need you, Gav. No one else can do the role justice."

"Stroking my ego?" Gavin asked with a laugh.

"Yeah. Is it working?"

"Probably. After I read it, I'll let you know if I'm interested."

"The script is winging its way to you as we speak."

"Okay. One thing. If I do like it, no fucking rewrites from the author. Understood? We do it as written, even if it means you don't get into his pants because he wants to 'improve' it and that's the trade-off to let him."

Chris laughed. "He is a she, so no worries in that department."

"Thank God," Gavin muttered as he booted up his computer and went online to check his email. "Okay, it's here. I'll get back to you after I've read it." He ended the call, then downloaded the file with the script and printed it out.

"I take it from what I overheard that they want you back," Mick said.

"Yep." Gavin put more paper in the printer feed when it let him know it needed it then leaned back, looking at Mick. "What about you? Any jobs on the horizon?"

"Two possibilities."

"Two? Damn." Gavin shook his head. "What's the world coming to when two people are looking for a hit man at the same time?"

Mick smiled wryly. "I know for a fact there's a lot more of them out there. I'm in a growth industry, Gav. It's much faster to hire someone to kill an enemy or a business rival or whatever than it is to try to work things out—at least in the minds of the people who want what I have to offer."

Gavin nodded. "Pretty much the same mindset as the people I ran cons on, I guess. Take the easy route rather than work for whatever it is you want."

"Exactly." Mick returned his attention to his laptop, drumming his fingers on the edge. Finally coming to a decision, he began typing, reread the email when he finished it then hit 'send'. Minutes later, he got a reply he needed then shredded the email before closing out of his account and shutting down.

"What happens if someone gets their hands on that?" Gavin asked, nodding at the laptop.

"First they'd need to enter the password before anything boots up. If they blow it, they're shit out of luck because they only have one shot at it. If they manage to get in, they have to get past the encryption on the hard drive. Any email I send or receive through my business account is also encrypted. Anything I want to save, which is damn little, isn't on the laptop. It goes to a remote cloud program run by my friend. Again, password protected and encrypted."

"Suppose you forget one of the passwords?"

"Short of knocking me over the head so I get amnesia, I won't. It's the way my mind is geared, just like you being able to learn and remember all the lines for a show you're in."

"That makes sense. Speaking of which..." Gavin gathered up the script, glad he'd remembered to tell the printer to collate the pages. "I'd better get to reading and see if this play is as good as Chris thinks it is. Given the last one he chose... Well, we'll see."

"Have at it. I have a couple of things I need to take care of."

"Then you might want keys and the security code if that means you're going out."

Mick grinned. "I could get in and out without them. I told you that. But yeah, it would save time if I did it legitimately. Oh, another thing—my bike. Since I'm staying here, what are the chances I can get a space for parking?"

"Not too hard since I have two of them. I'll let the building manager know you're using the other one so they don't try to tow it. It's the space to the right of mine."

Mick left after Gavin had made the call, given him his spare set of keys and the code. Then Gavin took the script into the living room, brewed a pot of coffee and settled down to read.

* * * *

Mick returned three hours later carrying several bags. When Gavin looked up questioningly, Mick held up one bag.

"Dinner." He headed to the kitchen to put the food he'd bought into the fridge. The other bags he deposited in his bedroom before going back to join Gavin.

"Got the script memorized yet?" Mick asked with a grin.

Gavin snorted. "Not hardly, but it is good so I'm probably going to take the role."

"Great. That'll keep you busy."

"While you go off to do your thing?"

"Yeah. It shouldn't take more than a couple of days."

"Flying or biking?" Gavin asked.

"Taking the bike."

Gavin nodded. "Then it's not on the other side of the Mississippi, or the mountains."

"Prying, Gav?" Mick replied with a frown.

"Just…interested. And yeah, I know you won't tell me anything. I wouldn't if I was you." Gavin leaned back, looking at Mick. "I was, however, going to offer my services to get you there and back, if you were going halfway across the country."

"Seriously?"

"Yep. I mean dropping you off somewhere would hardly let me know who you were targeting, unless you wanted to land in their house or office."

Mick chuckled. "That would be a bit obvious at best. Anyway, thanks for the offer but for this one I do need my bike. It gives me more mobility than a rental car."

"Riding it in a business suit might raise a few eyebrows."

"Not planning on…" Mick stopped, shaking his head. "You're too damned observant."

"Given that one of the bags you were toting was from Hugo Boss, probably the one at the mall, and that you have plenty of everyday clothes, it was a logical guess. Just like the fact that you also had a bag from a second-hand store. That tells me you're going undercover, for lack of a better word, in the opposite direction at some point. Let's see…" Gavin tapped his fingers together thoughtfully.

Mick watched him with a combination of wry amusement and worry. He wasn't used to anyone trying to figure out his game plan. *Hell, I've never put myself in a position where someone had the chance to. Am I stone-assed crazy to have done so now? More to the point, is he smart enough to work out what I have in mind?*

"Got it," Gavin said. "And you don't have to—probably won't—tell me if I'm right or not. But if it was me, and the man I was going after was a suit of some kind, I'd need to be able to tail him to get to know his daily habits. Thus what you bought at Boss. Then, since you don't want to take him out where he works or lives—I'm presuming—you need to become someone no one notices. To my way of thinking, that means either a laborer or a homeless person."

"I take it you took that play you walked out on to heart," Mick commented with a grin.

Gavin smiled broadly. "Nope. I ran across a site online created by a hit man."

"Oh, hell. I think I know which one you mean and someone should have shot him for doing that. Idiots have used his suggestions and have gotten caught, because they really didn't know what they were doing."

"Some people are born stupid, I guess."

"No shit," Mick muttered. He chuckled softly. "Maybe I should take you along on one of my hits and see how you'd fare."

"Badly, I'm sure. I don't know my ass from straight up about weapons, especially the sophisticated kinds I'm sure you use."

"Some are, yeah. But there are situations when a knife works better."

"If you say so. After all, you are the expert."

Mick nodded. "So I've been told."

"When do you leave?"

"I'll probably take off late tonight to avoid traffic. That gives us plenty of time to eat and fuck. Tension release and all that." Mick grinned at Gavin.

Gavin laughed. "You don't pull your punches."

"Do I have to?"

"Not with me, Mick. Not with me."

"Supper it is then..."

* * * *

"Strip. Now," Mick ordered.

"And if I don't?" Gavin retorted, pushing buttons. He could feel the tension rolling off Mick, even if his lover wasn't aware of it himself.

Mick grabbed Gavin's biceps painfully. "Are you defying me?"

Gavin lowered his gaze, shaking his head. "No," he whispered.

"Then do as you're told." Mick brought one hand down so hard on Gavin's denim-covered ass that Gavin felt as if he was already naked from the pain that ensued.

Gavin undressed so quickly that shirt buttons flew across the room when he tore it off.

"Better. Now me."

It took a second for Gavin to grasp what Mick meant. Then, with teasing slowness, knowing what would ensue, he started to take Mick's shirt off him. His instincts were correct.

A hard slap to his thigh, accompanied by, "You are trying my patience," told Gavin speed was the order of the night—at least for this.

"On your knees, on the bed, hands behind your back," Mick ordered.

Puzzled, Gavin did as he was told. A pause followed, then Mick bound Gavin's wrists together with a leather thong. When he'd finished, he snapped the ring on Gavin's cock and pushed him down until his face hit the pillow, leaving his ass in the air ready to be assaulted.

"You shouldn't defy me," Mick said. "You know what happens if you do." He delivered two swift, hard slaps to Gavin's naked butt.

Gavin bit down on his lip to keep from crying out.

"Good boy," Mick murmured, gently caressing where he'd just hit Gavin. Then he smacked him again and again, each one harder than the one before.

Gavin bit his lip so hard he tasted blood but he refused to make a sound. He heard the nightstand drawer open and knew what was coming next. His cock hardened further in anticipation. Suddenly Mick forced his lubed fingers through Gavin's entrance. The intrusion of three—not two—fingers was so unexpected Gavin let out a yelp of pain and surprise. Two fast slaps to his ass were his reward. One he needed. *Just a bit of a pain slut. More than a bit.* The thoughts flicked through his mind, even as he gripped his hands together to keep from crying out again.

Mick removed his fingers, instantly replacing them with the thick head of his swollen cock. He thrust in hard and fast. Gavin couldn't help it. He shouted as pain tore through him then bit down on the pillow to keep from doing so again.

"Shh, shh," Mick whispered unexpectedly. "It's what you *need*. What *I* need to give you."

He bent to brush a kiss at the nape of Gavin's neck. The tender moment ended as quickly as it had begun. Mick pounded into Gavin and soon pain grew into pleasure—pleasure so intense that if he could have,

Gavin would have exploded long before Mick finally came. At the last second, when Gavin was certain Mick was going to leave him hard and unsatisfied, his lover snapped off the cock ring. Unbelievable ecstasy flooded Gavin. Uncaring if he would be punished yet again, he cried out Mick's name as he came.

Chapter Seven

After their intense bout of sex, which had left Gavin aching and more than sated, he listened to Mick moving quietly around the condo. What Mick didn't know — what Gavin had no intention of telling him — was that he knew Mick had been playing him. The bags of clothes, the story that Mick was taking his bike with him — all lies.

Oh, he'll take the bike. I have no doubt about that. He'll take it as far as the airport, pick up a flight to wherever he's going and be back as promised two days from now thinking I'm none the wiser.

Gavin knew a con when he saw one. After all, he had been a past master at them. While he had to admire Mick for trying to pull one over on him, he had no intention of letting it slide. So when Mick went to retrieve some of his weapons from the panic room after dinner, Gavin added a small item to the bag Mick was taking with him. A tracking device left over from a con Gavin had pulled several years back. It might not be as sophisticated as the one Mick had put on Gavin's car but it would work.

As soon as he heard the condo's front door close, Gavin got out of bed. He dressed quickly then went into the media room to get the receiver for the tracker. He watched the red blip as it moved, going from where Mick had parked his bike, out of the lot and onto the street. Later, Gavin knew he'd called it right, so he pocketed the receiver, tossed a few items into a carry bag and teleported to The Admiral's Club on the upper level of the A Gates at DIA. He knew it would be empty at this hour of the night since it closed at eight and it was now almost three a.m.

From there, he took the train back to the main concourse, found a safe place to observe the area unseen and waited for Mick to appear. Half an hour later, Mick showed up, making it through security without any problems. Gavin let the tracker do its job and took the next train to the C Gates where he watched Mick head to the gate marked for a five a.m. flight to New Orleans.

That did not sit well with Gavin. The city was, after all, where the whole episode with Clemente had started. *In for a penny, in for a pound.* Gavin teleported to his house in New Orleans and found it vacant. It had been since he'd left it after Mira's death. Vacant but kept up, thanks to a cleaning company he paid to come in once a month to take care of it. He'd figured when he'd set it up that someday he might want to start using the house again — when things were settled with Clemente.

"I thought they had been," he muttered, stepping out onto the balcony overlooking the corner of Chartres and St. Philips. "If so, why is Mick coming here?"

An early morning breeze — smelling of oleander and magnolias mixed with the vague aroma of jambalaya

and gumbo wafting up from restaurants on Decatur —
ruffled his hair. He leaned on the railing, watching the
few straggling tourists making their way back to their
hotels, while the locals who held day jobs requiring
their presence at the crack of dawn walked past him
with takeout cups of coffee in hand.

He knew he should get some sleep. It would be at
least another six hours before Mick arrived, at which
point the man would have to get from the airport to
wherever he was staying. The problem was, Gavin
knew sleep wasn't an option right now. He was too
pissed and too worried, because there were only two
reasons he could think of for Mick's coming to NOLA.
One, he really did have a job. In that case, Gavin
would leave the way he had come without Mick being
any the wiser.

Two, for whatever misguided reason Mick had
decided to end Clemente's existence.

Drumming his fingers on the railing, he nodded
slowly before going back inside to make a call.

* * * *

Mick's plane landed on schedule at eleven-ten a.m.
He walked from the gate to baggage claim to retrieve
the bag containing his weapons that he'd checked
through. From there, he continued on to the rental car
agency where he had a reservation under an alias for
the car he'd use while he was in New Orleans. After
paying and getting the keys, he picked up the car,
tossed his bags in the trunk, then took off.

As he drove into the city, he went over his plan
again. He had the address he needed, and the tools to
do the job. The question was, would he actually be

able to kill Clemente or would Mick end up dead himself? Or worse?

It wasn't that he didn't trust that Magnus would try to deal with Clemente. But the younger vampire had obviously taken things into his own hands once in regards to Gavin. Mick wasn't willing to leave it to fate that Clemente wouldn't try again—overriding any orders from his Sire—to come after Gavin and finish what he'd started.

Am I being...stupid? Yeah, maybe. Am I going to try anyway? Yeah. I owe it to Gavin whether he'd think so or not.

When Mick arrived at the motel where he'd be staying for the duration, he checked in then went to his room. He unpacked, changed into black jeans, a gray, sleeveless hoodie and a pair of steel-toed Docs. He put a knife into the boot sheath, a stun gun that looked like a cellphone into its holster on his belt, and a five-inch tactical folder clipped inside the waistband of his jeans at the small of his back. Now if the knives had silver blades... He smiled briefly, sliding the last of his weapons into the hoodie's special interior pockets. He felt naked without any guns but this was not a job where one would really be useful unless it had silver bullets. It wasn't something he was willing to wait a week or more for his supplier to create with no guarantee that they'd fire correctly. The last item he added was a camera in a carrying case—his concession to looking like every other tourist in the city and a good repository for the tools he might need to bypass any security when he got to his destination.

As ready as he could be, he left the motel, heading for the house Clemente owned in the Garden District two blocks from Lafayette Cemetery. When he got close, he decided to park by the cemetery then stroll toward Clemente's place, snapping pictures of the large houses in the area in his guise as a tourist.

Clemente's house—two stories with tall white pillars going from the verandah to the roof on one side—sat enclosed by a tall, wrought iron fence with a padlocked front gate set between two wrought iron pillars. Another gate, also padlocked, barred the entrance to the driveway.

Guess he's not big on company. Mick surveyed the two sides he could see from where he stood, as the house took up a corner lot. He walked down to the next house. Its yard was much more accessible. Using the camera's telephoto lens, he checked the windows facing him in Clemente's house. There was no indication that anyone was watching, so he went up the driveway of the neighboring house until he found a safe spot to observe the back of Clemente's home.

He smiled when he realized there was a way to get into the backyard. What he'd assumed was a servants' entrance gate was virtually hidden by the vines that covered the back fence, a narrow path going past it from the street. He discovered, when he got to it, that the gate was merely locked, although there was a keypad beside it. He crouched by the fence, intending to wait ten to fifteen minutes to be certain the path wasn't a neighborhood shortcut from one street to the other.

When he was sure it was safe, he moved quickly to the gate and the keypad, taking out what he needed to bypass it. He had just finished and begun working on the lock when he sensed someone behind him. Tensing, he started to turn, reaching behind his back for his knife.

Before he could grab it, someone gripped his wrist and said, "You don't really want to do that."

Gavin paced the length of his bedroom and back again enough times that he almost expected to see he'd worn a path in the thick carpeting. After he'd placed his call, several hours earlier, he'd been told in no uncertain terms that he was to wait at the house. "Clemente would sense your presence in a heartbeat," had been given as the reason he had to stay where he was.

Did I do the right thing? Is Mick going to hate me for not trusting his...capabilities? His skills, as unlawful and...immoral as they may be? Like I should talk. Crime was my life for more years than I like to think about. I trusted my skills. Why the hell can't I – don't I – trust his?

Gavin knew the answers and it really had nothing to do with trust. It had to do with the fact that Mick was human and if Gavin was right, he was planning to go up against someone who was not human by any definition of the word.

Still, he knows what he's doing – at least to hear him tell it. And I have no reason not to believe him. If I was human, I'd be dead now. He almost smiled at that thought. *Given how old I am, I would definitely have died a long time ago, without Mick's putting a gun to my head.*

He left off pacing, going out to the balcony. The sun hung low on the horizon, its deep orange and almost blood-red light silhouetting the buildings and glimmering off the bit of the river he could see in the distance. *I pray that color doesn't presage the results of what Mick was planning.*

Resting his hands on the railing, he closed his eyes, trying to quell his guilt for bringing Mick into all that had happened in the first place.

"No guilt necessary. If it wasn't for him, Clemente would still be alive."

Gavin knew that voice and swung around. When he didn't see Brynja, he thought maybe his mind had been playing tricks on him to assuage his conscience.

She appeared seconds later in the bedroom. Immediately afterward, Torben teleported in with Mick. It shocked Gavin at how relieved he was to see them, especially Mick, even though the man scowled when he caught sight of Gavin.

"Didn't think I was up to handling it on my own?" Mick spat.

"Since I didn't figure out exactly what you had planned until it was too late and I know better than you what you were going up against..." Gavin replied, joining them in the bedroom.

"But it was my choice, not yours, damn it! I was prepared, and surprise, surprise, I knew better than to walk in on him after dark when he would be awake."

Before Gavin could reply, Brynja spoke.

"Both of you will be quiet and stop arguing this minute—that is an order. Gavin, Mick did what he thought was necessary to try to make certain Clemente would never threaten you again. Perhaps he was being foolhardy, but you cannot blame him for going after what he felt was the best solution. And you, Mick"—she turned her stern gaze on him—"do not be upset that Gavin cares enough to be afraid for you."

"He should have trusted me."

"If he had, you'd be dead now," Torben put in succinctly. "Not Clemente."

What Torben and Brynja had said finally sank in for Gavin. "Clemente is dead?"

"Yes," Mick replied. He managed a weak smile. "Not my fault, I'm afraid."

Brynja shook her head. "Without you it would not have happened, Mick." She turned to Gavin. "We arrived just as Mick was about to enter Clemente's domain. What I knew, and what he and Torben didn't, was that Clemente was aware that Mick was there. He was old enough he could awaken well before sundown." She smiled brightly. "I somehow neglected to inform Mick of this fact and allowed him to enter the house."

"Throwing me to the dogs. Or in this case the vampire," Mick muttered.

"It worked. While I had nothing to do with Clemente's death on a physical level, letting Mick enter did draw him out into the open. I read Clemente, saw that he had no inclination to stop his revenge on you, Gavin, despite his telling Magnus that he had given up on the idea. I'm afraid that Magnus was too trusting—again. He thought he'd dealt with his child and returned home." Brynja chuckled dryly. "Clemente would probably have been as good a confidence man as you were, Gavin, if he had decided to try his hand at it. Be that as it may, when he realized Mick was there, his first thought was to use him as a pawn against you by capturing and enthralling him. To instill in him the desire, the need, to kill you slowly and painfully while Clemente watched."

"Holy hell," Gavin whispered.

"Exactly. Being the good vampire that I am, I decided that for once I had to take a stand. I enthralled Clemente then allowed Torben to dispatch him."

"That didn't seem to sit too well with Mick," Torben said with a smirk.

"Damned right it doesn't!" Mick said tightly. "I still don't get why Torben and not me."

Brynja shook her head. "How many times do I have to say it? If you had killed Clemente, Magnus would have been forced to deal with you since you are human. He would have lost face by allowing a human to get away with killing his child."

"You vampires seem to have a thing about that," Mick grumbled.

Smiling, Brynja replied, "I'm afraid that as the most superior of the species, we do."

Torben shot Gavin a look that said she was crazy. "We" — he pointed to himself then to Gavin — "are the most superior species. Thank you very much."

"No," Mick said, deadpanning, "that would be the cockroach. They've been around since the beginning of time and they're impossible to get rid of."

"Are you saying we're lower than roaches?" Torben muttered.

Mick shrugged as he walked past the group and out to the balcony. "If the shoe fits…"

"You might want to talk to him," Brynja said softly to Gavin. "He's a male and not happy you didn't have faith in his abilities."

"If he had just—"

"Would you have told him, if the situation had been reversed?" she asked pointedly.

"Yeah, I…" Gavin sighed, shaking his head. "No, probably not."

"Then go out there and apologize, or something." She smiled softly. "I believe he did what he did because of his…his feelings for you, as much as he would probably deny it. Torben and I have reservations for dinner at Muriel's so we have to leave."

"We do? Oh, yeah, we do." Torben chuckled. "We'd ask you to join us but…"

"I have something more important to do." Gavin nodded, accepting what Brynja had said, although he was less than certain she was right. "Once again, thank you both for being here when I, no"—Gavin glanced at the lone figure standing on the balcony— "when *we* needed you."

"It was my pleasure," Brynja replied, kissing his cheek before she and Torben left the room. The proper way for once, Gavin noted with a trace of amusement.

Taking a deep breath, Gavin went out onto the balcony, leaning against the railing to look at Mick, who stared off into space.

"How pissed are you?" Gavin asked quietly.

"I'm trying to decide."

"I'm not sorry for bringing them in," Gavin told him. "I'd rather have you mad than dead."

"I knew what I was doing. Well..." Mick smiled ruefully. "I *thought* I had everything planned out until Brynja and Torben appeared. Even then, since she didn't actually try to stop me from going inside, I figured I was on the right track and they were just there as backup." He turned to lean against the railing beside Gavin, not looking at him as he said with apparent reluctance, "Thank you."

"For sending help, even if you didn't want it?"

"Yeah," Mick muttered.

"Think nothing of it. I just didn't want to lose a damned good bed partner."

For a second Mick seemed shocked. Then he burst out laughing. "I should punish you for being so flippant. And for thinking I'm *only* a bed partner."

"Me? Never," Gavin protested even as his libido jumped into high gear.

Mick raked his gaze over Gavin from head to toe before settling on the growing bulge behind the tight jeans Gavin wore. Then he pointed toward the bed, barely visible from where they were standing.

Gavin instantly headed to it, stopping just short of the edge.

"Strip," Mick ordered from the balcony doorway, his arms crossed over his muscular chest.

"Not unless you do," Gavin said defiantly.

Mick crossed the room with swift steps, gripping Gavin's shoulders hard. "This isn't a game, Gav. What you did, the lack of trust, hurt."

"You didn't trust me either," Gavin replied, not dropping his gaze from Mick's face.

"It had nothing to do with trust and everything to do with getting that bastard before he got to you. I wasn't willing to take the chance that he would."

"Why," Gavin asked softly. "Why weren't you willing to?"

"Because..." Mick hesitated. "Because," he whispered, "you're too im—" He obviously bit back what he was going to say. "You deserve to live without fear. I had to give you that chance. I knew, because I'm like him, that he wouldn't give up unless Magnus actually wiped his mind of any memories of you.

"You're not like him," Gavin replied adamantly. "You're not evil."

Mick snorted. "Tell that to the people I've killed. I'm as remorseless in what I do as he was in what he did."

"You're just doing a job that you're paid for. He did what he did because he enjoyed torturing people. Mira and anyone else he wanted to use for his purposes. That is true evil."

"There are shades of immorality? I didn't know that," Mick replied releasing his grip on Gavin.

"If I thought you were evil, not just somewhat immoral"—Gavin smiled a bit at that—"okay, definitely immoral. That's beside the point, however. If I thought you were evil I wouldn't have let you into my bed after the first time."

Mick arched an eyebrow. "When you used sex to bargain for your life?"

Gavin nodded. "After that... Well, I found I could deal, and I needed what you were offering. I still do."

"You have nothing to be afraid of now that Clemente's dead. So you don't need me to help you release your fear and tension."

"No," Gavin replied. "I just need you. Sex with you is exciting. Living with you is exciting." Resting his hands on Mick's hips, Gavin said, "Until you came along my life was..." Gavin shrugged. "Okay, don't take this the wrong way but I was bored."

"And now you have me to keep you entertained," Mick muttered, stepping away from him.

"No, damn it! Now I have someone to share things with. Sure, so far it's just been the Clemente problem, but I know there's more to both our lives than that."

"Yeah," Mick spat. "Speaking of which, aren't you supposed to be in Denver dealing with the show they want you for?"

"Technically, yes."

"Then why are you still here?"

"Because you are."

"That doesn't wash, Gav. We're..." He smiled ruefully. "We've become, maybe, friends with benefits as they say. I have no hold on you, any more than you have one on me, now that our business is finished."

Gavin scrubbed one hand through his hair. "I see," he said dispiritedly.

"Do you? I don't want to be tied down, no matter what I might have implied at one point. Which I don't think I actually did. With the life I lead, it's not an option."

"Fine. Go." Gavin pointed to the door. "It was fun while it lasted."

"Talk about clichés. That one's even worse than the ones in the play you walked away from."

"Is, isn't it?" Gavin managed a chuckle as he sank on the edge of the bed.

Mick nodded. "So, are you going to take the role in the new play?"

"It's a good one. I'm just not sure I want to continue acting."

"Well, from what you told me, you can afford to do nothing and still live quite well."

Gavin grimaced. "True, but…"

"But what, Gav?" Mick asked, sitting at the foot of the bed.

"I don't know. I wish I did. No, I take that back. I could be useful to you, if you'd trust me to keep my mouth closed about things."

"Oh, really? How do you figure?" Lying back, hands behind his head, Mick watched Gavin.

"In and out fast with no chance of being caught for one thing."

"Interesting idea," Mick replied thoughtfully. "That means you'd have to see the kill. Could you handle that?"

"I've seen people die before, Mick," Gavin said, his thoughts going to the death of his wife and his daughter.

"But have you seen them killed in cold blood? It's a whole different mindset."

"I lived through the Civil War."

"Not quite the same thing, but I'll give you points for that, I guess." Mick pulled Gavin down beside him "Do you really think you could handle it?"

"Won't know until I try."

"Gav, before you make a decision, you need to realize that if it's excitement you're craving this is not the way to get it. What I do is pretty mundane when it comes down to it. Go in, get the lay of the land, pick the right time and place, and *off* the target. Then get the hell away before shit happens."

"See," Gavin said, smiling, "you need me for that last part. Saves wear and tear on your nerves."

Mick chuckled. "I have nerves?"

"Probably not these days. Still, my point is valid."

"Yeah, it is," Mick replied seriously. "We'd make a hell of a team."

Gavin nodded. "I think so."

"Then you're in if you're sure you want to be." Mick grinned. "Except when we fuck, that is. Then I'm *in*" —he cupped Gavin's erection beneath the closure of his jeans—"and you deal."

"No problem with that," Gavin replied, putting his hand over Mick's.

Mick sat up suddenly, staring hard at Gavin. "Seems to me I told you a while ago to strip. Do it. Now."

"Damned bossy human," Gavin grumbled, getting off the bed so he could.

Mick smacked his ass. "And you like the hell out of it."

"I have to admit that I do. Never have before. But with you..." He paused thoughtfully for a moment while he finished undressing. "I never met someone I could really connect with after the death of my wife. Although I'm not sure she and I really connected when it comes down to it. It was a marriage of convenience and necessity. She needed someone to take care of her. I needed to hide the fact I was gay, because in my pack, my family, that was unacceptable and I did love and honor my parents. Anyway, in time, we grew to care for each other. Then she was killed."

Mick took Gavin's hands, asking with a trace of amusement laced with commiseration, "Why do we always seem to have deep conversations when we're getting ready to fuck?"

"A weird sort of foreplay? And if you don't get out of those clothes there's not going to be any fucking."

"Telling me what to do?" Mick said icily.

"No, Sir," Gavin replied, falling into his role, although he'd never called Mick Sir before.

"Good." Mick stripped off his shirt, began to undo his jeans then paused, snapping his fingers then pointing to the floor in front of him.

Gavin got the idea immediately. He dropped to his knees beside the bed and finished unzipping Mick's jeans to release his swollen cock. When Mick raised his hips, Gavin stripped the jeans the rest of the way off one-handed while holding Mick's cock tightly in his other hand. Then, without further ado, he took the swollen head between his lips.

"Enough," Mick growled, some moments later. "On the bed, on your hands and knees. Now!"

Gavin complied instantly, gripping the headboard. When Mick slapped his ass, hard, Gavin let out a yelp then bit back on another one when it happened again and Mick ordered him to remain silent. It was hard to keep quiet. Mick was being almost vicious with his hits. The only thing that gave Gavin the willpower to obey was telling himself that Mick needed to work out the last of his residual anger. Anger at Gavin for not trusting him.

When Mick was ready, he slammed into Gavin so hard that Gavin tasted blood when he bit down on his lip to suppress a shout of pain. But in the end, it was worth it. Pain became pleasure as it always did, and his climax, when it rolled through him, was the best he'd ever experienced, bar none.

"Are you all right?" Mick asked with a worried frown, seeing the blood on Gavin's lips. Using the corner of the sheet, he tried to wipe it away.

"Better than all right." Gavin replied, giving Mick a quick hug. "Not that I want to experience that level of pain every time, but damn…"

"I'm sorry. I was just…"

"I know what you were doing," Gavin told him, putting one finger to Mick's lips to silence him. "And I deserved it. But" —he stared hard at Mick—"next time you tell me what you're planning. No sneaking off thinking you're fooling me. Remember, I'm the experienced one when it comes to cons. You, young man, are very much an amateur, no matter what you may think to the contrary."

Mick chuckled. "Apparently so." He leaned back, smiling. "That could come in handy at times."

"You being bad at it?" Gavin asked with amusement.

"No. Damn. You being so good at it. I'm no slouch at casing out a target, but I have the feeling you could walk right into his home or business, get the lay of the land, and he'd think you actually belonged there, if you get what I'm saying."

"As a matter of fact, I do." Gavin stretched, licking the last trace of blood off his lip. "But let's discuss that later. For now, we could both use some sleep. Then, come morning, we can go back to Denver since everything you need is there at the moment."

"Sounds good to me."

Chapter Eight

Mick drummed his fingers on the edge of his laptop. "We won't know until we get there."

Leaning over his shoulder, Gavin studied the information Mick had on their next target. This would be the third job he'd worked with Mick. So far, he had found it interesting to say the least. Not the kill per se but all the planning that went into making it successful. "Agreed. But... Bring up his home address on the map site."

Mick was ahead of him and seconds later, he zoomed in on the Earth View of the property.

"Not ideal, but much better than the job site."

"Yeah, but at the site I'll have more freedom of movement."

"As you said, we won't know if either place will work until we get there to check them out in person, so let's move it."

Muttering "Yes, boss man," Mick shut down the laptop, then laughed when Gavin flipped him off. They packed what they needed to take with them, stowed their bags in the trunk of Gavin's new car, a very mundane 2010 Accord, and were on the road by midmorning.

Thirteen hours later, they were settled into a motel on the southern edge of Glendale, ten miles north of Phoenix.

"Not exactly the Ritz," Gavin commented as he unpacked.

"Don't knock it. It's air conditioned and right now that's what counts. That and the fact it's not too far from the construction site he's supervising."

"And close to a place where I can run. Want to come with?"

Mick glanced at the clock on the nightstand between the two beds and nodded, holding out his hand. Instantly they were in an area of low brush and cacti that they'd driven past on the way to the motel.

"Are you going to run with me?" Gavin asked. Grinning, he added, "You could use the exercise."

"Keep it down to a lope, and sure, why not? And I do not need to exercise, wise ass."

Gavin shifted, his clothes vanishing as his body took on its coyote persona. Then he looked up at Mick before taking off, staying in the moonlight so that Mick could safely keep up with him on the path Gavin had chosen. For a long time they ran, Gavin sometimes darting off to check out a small animal that interested him. Not that he'd do anything but watch it. He had a live and let live mindset when it came to the natural fauna in any place where he took on his coyote form. At one point, he heard Mick suck in a breath. Returning swiftly to the path, he saw what had Mick freezing in place. A large javelina blocked the way, looking back at Mick. Gavin yipped, catching the javelina's attention. For a moment, it seemed as if it would attack, then it turned and ran.

"That was one big pig, or whatever," Mick muttered. "Next time we do this I'm bringing a gun."

Gavin gave a hard shake of his head and from then on he stayed by Mick's side until they finished their run. After shifting back to his human form, Gavin teleported them back to the motel.

"When you come with me on a run," Gavin said firmly, "you will not bring anything more than a knife with you. Understood? The animals in the wild have as much right to be there as we do. Actually more than you do on some levels. They won't attack unless they're provoked."

"That, whatever it was, sure looked ready to take a piece of my hide—or yours."

"It was a javelina and that pose was more a 'keep away, I'm big and bad' than any intention of actually taking you on, unless you attacked first."

"And if I run into a bear or a wolf?"

Gavin chuckled. "I promise I won't take you anywhere where you would. I happen to like you without bites or claw marks."

"Me too," Mick muttered. "Me too."

* * * *

Mick and Gavin decided to check out the construction site first. It sat in the middle of nowhere with open land surrounding it on three sides and a six-lane highway abutting the fourth side.

"You'll be hard pressed to get close enough to take him out without someone seeing you," Gavin said as they studied it from their vantage point in the parking lot of a fast-food place across the highway from the site.

"Unfortunately, you're right." Mick snickered softly. "Especially since they have a sign at the gate stating 'No weapons allowed'. I have the feeling that includes me."

"No shit," Gavin agreed.

Mick lifted his binoculars again, scanning the site. "Got you," he muttered, focusing on an older man wearing a hardhat, slacks and a blue shirt. He was talking to several of the construction workers and it was fairly obvious from the frowns on their faces that what the man was saying didn't sit well with his crew. Then one of the men said something, the target replied, and the mood swiftly changed, most of the workers smiling as they headed off to the building under construction.

Now just what did he tell them? Not that it matters. Or won't soon. Mick studied the target when the man walked over to a guy in a suit and hardhat standing by the entrance to the site. They talked for a few moments, the businessman—if that's what he was— nodding several times. Then they went into one of the construction trailers.

"I'd give my eye teeth to know what they're talking about," Mick said.

"Want me to find out?" Gavin asked.

Mick shook his head. "Even if you shifted, you'd still stand out like a sore thumb in there. Besides which, knowing wouldn't change anything. I'm here to kill him, not spy on him and report back on what I find out. Okay, next stop his house."

The target's home, a sprawling fieldstone ranch-style house, set in the center of at least two acres of land in Mick's estimation. A cream brick wall surrounded the property with two wide wooden gates breaking its expanse, one in front and one at the rear. From where they were standing, on the side of a hill behind the house, Mick could see a wide patio and a large swimming pool that no one was taking advantage of despite the early afternoon heat.

"This man's not poor by any stretch of the imagination," Gavin commented, focusing his binoculars in on the gatehouse by the back gates. "Looks like he has his own security guards." He handed the binoculars to Mick. "Hang on, I'll take a closer look."

"Just don't get shot," Mick cautioned, knowing what Gavin had planned.

"I'll try not to."

Mick watched as, moments later, Gavin in his coyote form loped down the hillside to the brick wall and paused along one side of it. He smiled when he saw the coyote vanish, only to reappear in the yard, under a tree next to the patio. Gavin disappeared from view again. The next time Mick saw him, he stood by the back door to the house, the bushes surrounding the patio effectively hiding him from the gatehouse. Then he was gone.

Mick jumped slightly when Gavin showed up beside him several minutes later, shifting back to his human form.

"No pets, which is good," Gavin told Mick. "But there are two dogs in an outbuilding next to the garage."

"Aren't dogs pets?"

"In this case I'm betting they're guard dogs. Probably let out at night. The men at the gates are armed. The security system on the house, from what I could see of it without going inside, is primo."

Mick smiled tightly. "Once again, I'm glad you're working with me. You just saved me several hours of surveillance." Mick thumbed toward the path leading to where they'd left the car. "Let's grab something to eat, then go back to the site and follow the guy when he leaves. I need to know if he's the kind who goes straight home, or if he stops off for drinks or a quick roll in the hay, first."

* * * *

Mick and Gavin spent the next two days keeping track of the target's movements, looking for a pattern that would give Mick the best opportunity to do what he was being paid for. They found it the second day. The first evening after leaving the site, the target was accompanied by a pair of men who looked like construction workers but from their attitudes, as Mick pointed out, they were obviously bodyguards. The trio of men went to the target's company headquarters and from there to a gym located halfway between his company and his home. The pattern was repeated the following day, and now, on the third day, the target and his guards were once again pulling into the lot behind the gym.

Mick drummed his fingers on the car's dashboard. "Let's find someplace to park over there." He pointed to a busy restaurant a block away.

With a nod, Gavin drove to the restaurant and found a parking space in a far corner of the back lot, next to a large dumpster. "Where are you going to set up?" he asked Mick.

After a moment's consideration, Mick replied, "On the roof of that apartment building." As he spoke, he got out of the car, waited for Gavin to pop the trunk, then took out the rifle case he'd brought with him. He closed the lid just as Gavin joined him.

Seconds later, they were on the roof, next to the housing for a swamp cooler.

Mick commented as he put the rifle together, "You sure save me wear and tear on shoe leather."

Gavin chuckled softly, inched to peer over the edge of the roof then checked the time. "We have an hour if he holds true to form."

Mick nodded. "Did you bring a book to read?" he asked with a grin.

"Nope. But..." Gavin flipped open his phone and brought up a word game. "Best two out of three pays for dinner."

Mick moved closer to him, positioning himself so he could keep an eye on the back door of the gym. They played two games and were in the middle of the third when Mick saw the door to the gym open and the target's two guards come out. Gavin immediately closed his phone and hunkered while Mick, rifle in hand, crawled toward the edge of the roof.

The guards stood for a moment, obviously scanning the lot and the rooftops across from it. They turned to beckon to Mick's target. By the time the man joined them, Mick was in place. He sighted in on the man, pulled the trigger once then again. Both shots hit home, one in the target's chest, the other in his gut. Before the guards could react, Gavin stood beside Mick with the rifle case. Instantly, they appeared behind their car, the dumpster hiding their sudden appearance from anyone who might have been looking in that direction.

Gavin used the key fob to unlock the car doors, they both got in, and while Gavin pulled the car out of the parking lot and onto the street, Mick broke the rifle down, replacing the parts in the case. As they drove away, the sound of sirens rent the air. Soon a police cruiser tore past them, lights flashing, and when Mick turned to look, he saw it wheel into the drive beside the gym before disappearing from view.

* * * *

"You owe me dinner," Mick said late the following afternoon after they'd arrived back at the condo and unpacked.

"The hell I do. I was winning the third game."

Mick snorted. "But it was my turn next and I had all the letters I needed for a triple play."

"Dreamer," Gavin muttered, going to the kitchen to get a couple of bottles of water. He tossed one to Mick.

"Nope, I would have won. So"—Mick grinned—"where are you taking me?"

Gavin thought for a moment. "Do you like barbecue?"

"Yeah."

"Good. Go change into something comfortable."

Mick arched an eyebrow. "How comfortable?"

"Casual. Where we're going is not hoity-toity by a long shot."

"Whew, because I have only one good suit here." Mick smiled wryly. "The one I bought to try to fake you out about a job when I was actually heading to New Orleans."

"Which you have never worn. Maybe I should change my plans and take you somewhere fancy."

"Umm... No?" Mick hustled out of the kitchen, going to change from his black 'work' clothes into jeans and a dark green shirt. He came out of his bedroom to find that Gavin had changed too, into jeans and a green shirt. "Hell, we're going to look like..."

"Twins?" Gavin laughed. "Hang on." He left, coming back a minute later wearing a red shirt. "Better?"

"If you don't mind us looking like a couple on a bad Christmas card, then yeah. So are we taking my bike or the car?"

"Neither." Gavin gripped Mick's shoulder and seconds later, they stood beside a dumpster in an alley between two stand-alone buildings. Gavin led the way around one to what Mick at first thought was a gas station. Then he saw the sign over the door.

"We're in Oklahoma?"

"Nope. Kansas City. At the best barbecue restaurant in the city, bar none."

They entered to find a line of people from the front door to the order counter at the far side of the room. "It better be good if you expect me to stand in line for an hour to get my dinner."

It actually took them about twenty minutes. By the time they'd ordered and had found an empty table in a back corner of the room, Mick's mouth watered. "If this tastes as good as it smells..." He took a large bite of the pulled-pork sandwich, moaned in appreciation and wiped some sauce off his chin.

Gavin was a bit neater while eating his Smokie Joe, a combo of smoked beef and pork. But then he hadn't poured on a ton of extra sauce the way Mick had.

"How the hell did you find this place? And can we move to KC so we can come here every night?" Mick asked when he finally took a break from eating.

Gavin laughed. "You know we can come here any time without moving to KC. As to how I discovered it, I was out here about eight years ago doing what I did best at the time. The man I was dealing with brought me here one evening and it was love at first sight. Or rather at first taste."

"I'm guessing what you did best means running a con," Mick said acidly.

Gavin looked at him in surprise. "Of course. What else?"

Taking a deep breath, Mick replied, "Nothing. Sorry."

Leaning forward, his elbows on the table, Gavin said, "Talk to me."

Mick hesitated. "Okay. Remember the guy I told you about. The one who ratted me out? Well he claimed I was his best and only friend and the only man he let screw him. Turned out he had a lucrative sideline whoring. Maybe he didn't consider his johns as friends but... Anyway, when I found that out, we had a major blowup. That's why he tried to rat on me to the cops."

"So you jumped to the conclusion from what I said that I was using sex as part of the con I was running. I'll tell you here and now, I never did that. Not with anyone. Ever."

"I believe you. I don't know why it would matter anyway."

"Because you're human and we're in a relationship of sorts."

Mick chuckled. "You're saying if I wasn't a human it wouldn't bother me if I found out you used sex to con someone?"

"Dear God, no. I meant you're only human... Okay, that doesn't work either. You're a living being with emotions and feelings and..."

"Stick with human, Gav. I was only kidding." He leaned back, studying his lover. "We make a good team and I'm not about to let anything end that. So I had a bit of *déjà vu* about the bastard and how I felt when I found out what he was doing. It won't happen again."

"More to the point if it does, or if something else sets you off kilter, tell me straight out. Considering what we do, keeping things from each other is not a good thing."

"Absolutely." Mick glanced around. "And we might want to continue this discussion, if we're going to, somewhere else. I don't think anyone close to us can overhear us, as noisy as this place is, but..."

"Good point. So finish up and we'll take a walk to work off dinner. Or more, I'll take you to a place I found that helped keep me sane while I was here."

A few minutes later Mick watched Gavin in dismay. "What the hell do you think you're doing?"

"Walking along the wall?"

Mick leaned over the low stone wall, peering down at the Missouri river far below them. "If you fall you'll break your damned neck. Besides which, you're not some ten-year-old kid anymore. Stop acting like one."

"Come join me. Or are you chicken?" Gavin said, grinning slyly as he continued along the wall.

"I'll show you chicken." Mick jumped up behind Gavin, teetering momentarily before he got his footing. They walked a few yards then Mick paused, looking across the river. "Damn, some view."

"Is, isn't it? And from where we're standing, it makes me feel like Lewis and Clark. Sort of."

"What do they have to do with anything?"

"Come on, I'll show you." Gavin jumped down, waited for Mick to join him then led the way to a statue that depicted the famous explorers with two of their companions and Lewis' dog, Seaman.

"You were right," Mick said as he studied the sculpture and then the park. "This is a very peaceful place even with people wandering around."

"Now let me show you another one that I like," Gavin replied, taking hold of Mick's arm.

The next thing Mick knew they appeared in a small stand of pine trees with dirt beneath their feet. A pavilion sat a few yards away and off one side, a low rock and grass-covered mound. He turned and saw buildings across a wide avenue. "Where the hell are we now?"

Gavin laughed. "About two miles from home."

"You're shitting me."

"Nope. Come on, let's do what you said and walk off dinner." Gavin waved his arm, indicating the paths through the park.

"I think that was you who said it then we did. In KC."

"So we'll finish off here and hike back home."

"Remember," Mick grumbled, although he smiled too, "human here. I don't have your stamina."

Gavin just grinned before he reminded Mick that he seemed to have lots of stamina when they were in bed together.

"Yeah, but that's different. That's fun."

"And walking isn't?"

"Well..." Mick sighed. "Okay, lead the way. Never let it be said I can't keep up with a coyote in disguise."

"Maybe I should shift and find out."

"Gav..." Mick shook his head. "I think that would cause real problems unless I put a collar and leash on you. Then, maybe, you'd pass as my pet." He tapped his lips pensively. "Hmm..."

"Do not even think it," Gavin said firmly. "I do not take well to being collared. No matter the reason."

"I wouldn't. Not really. That's not a kink I'm into, believe it or not."

Gavin hugged him quickly before starting to walk again. "I didn't think it was."

"On the other hand, next time we go to my place, remind me to grab my cuffs." Mick grinned when Gavin visibly swallowed, a look of anticipation on his face. Leaning in, Mick whispered, "They beat the hell out of the thongs we've been using."

In seconds, they arrived in the bedroom at Mick's house.

"Where are they?" Gavin asked as he began to strip. "Cuff me and—"

"And fuck you?" Mick grinned. He found the cuffs then stripped as well. "On the bed, now, your ass toward me," he ordered. "Hands there." Mick pointed to the corners of the metal headboard.

When Gavin quickly complied, Mick cuffed Gavin's hands to the uprights where they met the crossbar. Then he stepped back, smiling wickedly. "I like you in cuffs. Very...sensual."

"Sensual?" Gavin snorted softly.

"Now you know better than to make a sound at this point." Mick smacked Gavin's ass. Much to his surprise, he realized it was just that—a smack. He meant to show Gavin who was in charge, but not with any desire to inflict real punishment. *Am I getting soft in my old age, or is it because, for once, we're...playing instead of working out anger or fear or a need to...to atone for something?* Whatever the reason, Mick was unwilling to inflict intense pain this time. Yes, he'd hurt Gavin. That was part of who they both were when it came to sex. But he'd do it because it's what turned them on. He slapped Gavin's ass again and once more he savored the faint hiss of pain from his lover. "You like that, don't you?"

Gavin nodded but didn't reply.

"You have permission to answer," Mick told him.

"You know I do," Gavin murmured, his words barely above a whisper.

"What?" Mick brought his hand down hard on Gavin's butt.

"You know I do," Gavin said more forcefully. "It... You..."

"Yes?"

"It lets me know you...care. About my pleasure as well as your own."

Mick almost replied, "About you," but restrained himself. Was it the truth? Probably on some level. But he wasn't willing to let Gavin know. Caring caused problems he wasn't willing to deal with.

Taking the lube from the nightstand drawer, Mick oiled three fingers, thrusting them into Gavin's waiting entrance. He found Gavin's gland and stroked it, telling him in no uncertain terms he was not to come until given permission. Then he tormented his lover unmercifully until he knew Gavin was on the verge of disobeying his order.

Pulling his fingers out, he pressed the well-lubed head of his cock against Gavin's hole and thrust in hard, burying his cock to the balls in one deliberate movement. Gavin cried out, his knuckles turning white as he gripped the headboard. Mick rewarded his vocalization with a swift hit to Gavin's thigh before pounding into him. His own restraint was sorely tested as he waited for Gavin to start begging that he be allowed to come, wondering if he would.

"Please..." Gavin moaned.

Mick pulled almost out then thrust in again, exploding. He barely managed to say, "You may come," before the intensity of his orgasm took his breath away. Gavin shuddered once before he came with a cry that echoed through the bedroom.

Chapter Nine

"This one is not going to be easy," Mick said, turning from his laptop to look at Gavin.

"When are they?"

"When I can point a gun or use a blade, and walk away. And with you in my corner, I don't even have to walk away anymore."

"So what makes this one different?"

"It has to look like an accidental death."

"So we shove him or her down a flight of stairs or in front of a moving car."

"First off, there's no guarantee that'll do the trick. Second, from what the client told my friend, they want to collect double indemnity from the target's death and it has to look like the accident happened at the target's place of work."

Gavin booted up his computer and went online. After finding the site he needed, he read the information, relaying it to Mick. "A double indemnity clause covers any accident, including murder by a person other than, and not in collusion with, the beneficiary of the insurance policy. Also, it can't be suicide or a death caused by the victim's own gross negligence, or from natural causes."

Mick frowned, rereading the details in the order for the hit. "The guy is the co-owner of a restaurant. Presumably with the person who wants him dead although, of course, it doesn't say as much."

"So the client wants the whole enchilada but the target isn't willing to sell his half to him, or something along those lines."

"Yeah, probably. That means the death has to look accidental." Mick smacked his forehead. "Well, duh, dummy. That's what it says here." He tapped the screen.

"Why does it have to happen at the restaurant?"

"You got me, but that's one of the specifications. Maybe because the client will be working there too and it'll give him a free and clear alibi if the cops question that it was an accident."

"What kind of accidents happen at restaurants?"

"He falls into the deep fryer," Mick replied with a grin. "He slips and falls, stabbing himself to death with the knife he's holding. It's a fancy restaurant and a chandelier falls on him."

"Mick, get serious."

"Hey, I read about a chandelier falling thing online a couple of years ago."

"Knowing you, I don't doubt it, and that you filed the information away for future reference. However, I think we'd be hard pressed to make it happen without injuring other people in the process."

True. Same with rigging some sort of explosion like with one of the restaurant's stoves if they're gas."

"Okay." Gavin glanced back at the information he'd found. "Double indemnity does cover murder."

"Yeah, but as you said, it can't point back to our client. And a straight out hit would, unless the cops are dumber than fence posts."

Gavin chuckled. "Which we can't count on, I'm afraid."

After a moment's thought, Gavin snapped his fingers. "A robbery. An armed robbery."

"Hmm." Mick nodded slowly. "That could work. It would fill the stipulation of the target's being murdered and cover the client's ass if he's on the premises at the time it happens."

"I wonder if the client realizes he's giving us his identity by having us set this up at the restaurant."

"That's assuming it is the target's partner. It could be someone else who works there. Maybe a scorned lover or an employee he's raked over the coals one too many times. Or even a disgruntled customer."

"True enough," Gavin agreed. "Sorry, sir, but we won't comp your meal just because it turned out you don't like the way we make our spaghetti sauce."

Mick shook his head, trying not to laugh, and returned his attention to the email from his friend. After memorizing all the pertinent information, he eradicated the mail, sent an encrypted one back saying he'd take the job but at double his normal fee, and sent it off.

"Now we wait and see if the client accepts my terms," he told Gavin, after explaining what he'd done.

* * * *

Mick's client was more than willing to pay double for the successful elimination of the target. After due consideration and weighing the pros and cons, Mick, with Gavin's agreement, decided the idea of pulling the holdup early in the evening was their best option. So, forty-eight hours later, they parked a rental car in a space in front of Cuisine Royale. Before that, during the afternoon, they had staked out the restaurant. As Gavin had pointed out, not that Mick wasn't aware of the fact, they had to make certain that their target was doing what they expected—hosting or being the cashier at the desk by the front door.

They had rented the car, under an alias, with the intention of using it for their getaway then dumping it a few blocks from the restaurant, after which Gavin would teleport them home. Given that they were doing the hit in front of witnesses, Gavin couldn't just whisk them away once the target was dead.

Mick scanned the sidewalk, waiting for the right moment to leave the car and enter the restaurant. Thanks to Gavin's skills with makeup, neither man looked like themselves. As an added precaution, they both wore latex gloves and billed caps pulled low over their foreheads.

"Ready?" Mick asked as he gripped the passenger side handle.

"Yep." Gavin opened his door, stepping out onto the sidewalk, then headed across the pavement when Mick joined him.

They walked into the restaurant and up to the target standing at the cashier's desk. The man looked at them with disdain, as they obviously didn't meet the 'dress code' for the place, and asked, "Two of you for dinner?"

"Nope," Mick replied quietly, shifting to hide the pistol he pulled from the holster under his jacket so that only the target could see it. "Two of us relieving you of the contents of the register. Open it slowly and don't make any foolish moves when you do."

The man did as he was ordered, his face ashen with fear.

"He's going for a weapon," Gavin spat as planned.

"Should have listened to me," Mick told the target when he fired, hitting the man in the chest.

"Freeze. Drop the gun, hands behind your heads. Now!"

Mick turned, saw two police officers with their guns trained on him and Gavin, and started to do as they ordered.

Gavin apparently had a different idea and Mick instantly knew what it was. "No, they'll—" Mick exclaimed as Gavin closed the distance between them, grabbing Mick's arm. At the same moment both officers fired, Mick heard a gasp of pain then he and Gavin arrived in the condo.

"Guess we're not cut out to be armed robbers," Gavin managed to say before he collapsed, blood from his wounds pooling on the floor.

"Fuck! Damn it, Gav!" Mick kneeled beside him, tearing off Gavin's jacket and shirt to assess the damage. "God damn it, don't you die on me," he growled when he saw that one bullet had torn through Gavin's shoulder and the second shot had ripped into Gavin's side. Leaping to his feet again, he raced into the bathroom, peeling off his latex gloves along the way. After grabbing towels from the rack and washcloths that he quickly dampened, he returned to the living room, stopping in shock when he saw a badly wounded coyote lying where Gavin had been just moments before. Kneeling again, pressed the towels to both wounds to keep the animal from bleeding out. To his surprise, he realized the bleeding had slowed to a bare trickle. Then, even as he watched, it stopped.

"What the hell?" he muttered as he used the wet clothes to clean the blood off the coyote's fur, revealing two bullet holes, one in the animal's side, one in his shoulder. Holes that were, if Mick could believe what he was seeing, starting to close. Shaking his head incredulously, he muttered, "Another perk of being a shifter?" Uncertain what to do but knowing he couldn't leave the coyote lying in his own blood, Mick carefully picked him up, carrying him into Gavin's bedroom. He set him gently on the floor just long enough to put a folded blanket from the closet over the bed's comforter. Then he laid the coyote on it.

"So do I call a vet, or a doctor?" he asked, stroking the coyote's muzzle. He knew he really couldn't call anyone. After all, how would he explain having a wounded coyote in a bedroom in the middle of the city? And if Gavin shifted back before a doctor came, trying to explain bullet wounds would only have the guy reporting them to the cops.

So I wait it out and hope to hell he doesn't die on me.

Unwilling to leave Gavin until he was certain that wouldn't happen, Mick got onto the bed beside him. Resting one hand on the coyote's chest, Mick could feel the slow rise and fall of his breathing and soon his own breathing deepened to match Gavin's and he slept.

* * * *

Someone shook Mick's shoulder and his eyes flew open. Gavin looked at him with a trace of amusement as he said, "Wake up, sleepyhead."

"Are you all right?" Mick asked, bolting erect to look at him.

"I feel like hell, but yeah, I'm alive."

"Damn, Gav. You scared the shit out of me. How you managed to get us back here…"

"Determination. I don't like being caged."

"I'm not too partial to that idea myself. Still…" Then Mick frowned. "I wonder how the cops are going to explain our sudden disappearance."

"Smoke and mirrors," Gavin told him with a brief smile. "Yeah, it was probably a stupid move on my part but I can blame it on being in pain. And not the kind that I like."

Mick barely smiled at that and replied, "I gather shifters heal pretty fast, but damn, those were hellish wounds and now they're gone."

"Mostly gone. Still healing the damage inside, though shifting and sleeping definitely sped up the process. It always does." Gavin grimaced as he started to get out of bed.

Mick put his hand on Gavin's uninjured shoulder to stop him. "Where the hell do you think you're going?"

"The bathroom?"

"Ah, well…" Mick watched him carefully as Gavin moved slowly to the door, ready to leap to his assistance if it looked as if his friend might collapse.

When Gavin came out, Mick took his turn. He discovered when he entered the bedroom again that Gavin wasn't there. The sound of the TV led Mick to the living room. Gavin sat flicking through the channels, stopping at each news report. He finally found the one he wanted, glancing up at Mick and pointing.

"One minute the killers were there, the next they were gone," the cop that the reporter was interviewing said. "It was pandemonium and... Well... They must have taken advantage of the people rushing up to help the man they shot and...vanished."

"I wonder if he believes what he's telling her," Mick said, sitting beside Gavin.

"Probably on some level," Gavin replied. "It's his way of explaining the unexplainable, especially to himself. Mind over matter." He returned his attention to the news report.

"According to others on the scene," the reporter stated, "two men dressed in jeans, jackets over work shirts and baseball caps entered Cuisine Royale, going to the cashier's desk. One man, described as having a blond mustache and a small scar on his forehead, pulled a gun, ordering the cashier to give them the money in the register."

Mick automatically touched his forehead when he heard that, shaking his head. "I'd better get rid of the scar and shave."

"Might be a good idea," Gavin agreed.

"You still have traces of makeup you missed when you washed your face," Mick pointed out.

The reporter went on. "The second man appeared to be of Hispanic descent with long, black hair tied back with a thong. Both men were described as in their mid to late thirties."

Gavin rubbed a finger along the underside of his jaw, nodding in reply to Mick's suggestion when he saw brownish makeup on his finger.

The news story ended with the reporter saying that there was a full manhunt in progress for the two killers and that the police were warning the public that the men should be considered armed and dangerous.

"What I don't get is how the cops showed up so fast," Gavin said after clicking off the TV.

"Three guesses, and the first two don't count. The whole thing was a setup and if I find the bastard who did it, his ass is mine."

"Ours," Gavin said succinctly.

"Yeah. I wonder if the client even knew the man we killed or if he just picked the restaurant out of a hat for the job. Then watched the joint and called the cops to tell them he'd gotten a tip that someone was going to rob the place when we got there."

"We won't know until we find him. Whoever he is, he knew what he was doing as far as making his story sound plausible to us."

Mick smiled dryly. "He had to. He knew who he was going up against."

"How could he? I mean the only person who knows your name is your friend who acts as your intermediary. To anyone he sends your way, you're just a hired killer. No name, no face, no anything to let the client know who you are, any more than you know who they are."

"There's no fucking way he'd rat me out. No way, no how."

"Mick, if it was a setup and not just dumb luck on the cops' part that they were in the right place at the right time, it almost has to be him."

Leaning back, Mick stared up at the ceiling. "Johnny has three men he handles."

"A name for your friend. Finally."

"Yeah. Johnny Morgan. Sorry 'bout that. I've just got used to calling him my friend since I mentioned him to you the first time. Anyway, I wonder..." Mick went into the media room, returning with his laptop. Opening it, he went online and, after due consideration, typed an email. Then he encrypted it before sending it through the usual secure channels to his friend.

When he got no reply after waiting over an hour, he made a phone call.

* * * *

"What the hell do you mean he's dead?" Mick glared daggers at the woman who had given him the news about Johnny Morgan.

Mick had had Gavin teleport them to the building housing the small office Johnny Morgan ostensively rented in the downtown area of Chicago. Mick had visited there only once, back when he'd first met Johnny, but he knew that his friend owned not only the office but the whole building through a holding company.

The woman—Diana Walsh, Johnny's secretary in what was a one-man private investigation agency— backed away from Mick's anger. "It happened three days ago. He was"—she took a deep breath, apparently trying to rein in her emotions—"he was supposed to go meet a new client. He called me to tell me the person must have given him the wrong address, because no one there knew who he was talking about. That's the last thing I heard from him. An hour later, two policemen showed up here. Johnny... A hit-and-run driver"—she gulped— "Johnny died at the scene."

Finally, Ms. Walsh seemed to realize she had no idea who Mick was. "Are you...? Were you one of Johnny's clients?"

Deciding to be at least partially truthful, Mick replied, "No, I'm an old friend of his from way back.

We kept in touch on and off and since I was in the city I decided to drop by to see him."

"I wish…" She sighed. "You got here just in time for his funeral. Once that's over, I'm closing the office. I don't know why I even kept it open except… I guess I figured some of his clients might want the files he kept on them."

"Have they?"

"A few. Yes. After the funeral I'll have the remaining records shredded then that's it."

"No one inherited the business?"

"No. You have to know he had no living relatives if you're his friend. A lawyer came by yesterday to tell me that."

"Did he say if there were any heirs to Johnny's property?"

"No. But then that's not really my business. He just informed me that the office would be closed and the building would go up for sale."

"You knew Johnny owned the building before the lawyer told you?"

She nodded. "He and I had a casual relationship outside of work. He told me one time when he was feeling…chatty."

"Johnny? Chatty?"

Ms. Walsh smiled sadly. "Not often but…"

"Sounds like him. Kept everything close to his vest unless he knew you well." Mick patted her shoulder. "I'm sorry for sounding as if I was grilling you. That wasn't my intention. I guess I'm still in shock myself. When is the funeral?"

"Tomorrow morning at ten, at Mount Greenwood Cemetery. There isn't going to be a church service first."

"Thank you. We'll be there."

"Now what?" Gavin asked when they were back on the street.

"Damned good question. We know, or at least I'd be willing to bet, that Johnny was murdered. That was just a bit too fortuitous. He's killed then we almost get busted two days later. Someone is out to stop us."

"*Us* meaning Johnny and the three of you he handled."

"Exactly."

"Do you have any clue who the other two are?"

"No. But I wouldn't be surprised if they show up at the funeral tomorrow if they know what's going down."

"If the same thing happened to them that did to us, you know they will. If, of course, they're still alive and not in jail."

"There is that." Mick smiled at Gavin. "If it wasn't for you, I'd definitely be in jail now, or worse if those cops got trigger-happy."

"Which they did," Gavin rubbed his shoulder. "I feel sorry for the guy you shot. It wasn't his fault he got targeted."

"Agreed. So we're going to avenge his death too, when we find the man responsible for all of this. Right now, though, we should go back to the hotel and come up with a plan of action," Mick said, as they headed back to the lot where they'd left the rental car.

* * * *

"Even if the other two men Johnny handled do show up at the funeral, how will you know?" Gavin asked as he paced the hotel room.

"That, my man, is a good question. Something in their expression. The way they hold themselves."

Mick knew it was safe to talk about their problem, because he'd done what he always did when he and Gavin had to stay at a hotel. He'd used the best device available to make certain the room wasn't bugged then set up an audio jammer as a final precaution.

"The dead look in your eyes you get when you're about to take out a target."

"Yeah," Mick replied automatically. Then he frowned. "I do?"

"You do. It's as if you aren't seeing anything except the spot where the bullet will hit. You blank out the target's face and everything else about him."

"I suppose so. It's the kill that matters at that point, and how to accomplish it cleanly."

"And ignore the fact they're a living, breathing human being."

Mick shrugged. "At that point, they aren't. Or won't be within seconds." He looked at Gavin, frowning. "Are you starting to have second thoughts about what we do?"

"Not really. I guess it just hit me, after getting shot, that being a target is not exactly a pleasant experience. Not that I'm empathizing. As you said at one point, you do what you're hired for, because if you didn't, someone else would. Whoever hires you thinks the target deserves what they're getting and who are we to argue?"

"Exactly. If the man I killed at the restaurant was an actual target—and that's pretty doubtful now—he must have done something to piss off my client. Since we don't know which one was in the right, we just do what we're paid for and walk away."

"True enough." Gavin smiled, adding, "Just like I did when I conned some sucker out of a large portion of his money. If he was stupid enough or greedy enough to fall for it, he got what he deserved and I became a lot richer as a result."

"You know… Some people would look at the two of us and say we have no morals."

Gavin laughed. "Some people would be right. Anyway, back to the original discussion. How are we going to figure out if anyone going to Johnny's funeral is another killer for hire like you?"

"As I said, how they hold themselves, the way they watch everyone else who's there. They'll be doing the same thing we'll be doing, looking for the other two men Johnny handled. And, more importantly, just like us, they'll be looking for the guy who dusted Johnny and is after us."

"What if it's one of them?"

"Who set this up? Now that's something I never considered."

"Then do. As strange as it may seem, I can see one of them"—Gavin spread his hands—"finding religion, for lack of a better word…"

"And deciding what we do is wrong?" Mick shook his head, going to stare out of the window. Not that he didn't think that was possible, because he supposed it was. Instead he wondered if any one of them would be stupid enough to go up against the other two. He turned back to Gavin and said as much.

"Do you think you could take out one of them if it came down to it?" Gavin questioned.

"Possibly. Probably. If I had good reason to."

"Would you do it one on one, or set him up the way we were set up?"

"Hell, you should know the answer to that by now. I'd go after him. No game playing."

"Good. Because if it is one of them, that's what you're going to have to do. Oh, and it just occurred to me," Gavin said, "that we might also add another thing to look for on your list. Someone who seems surprised to see you're still running free."

"Nope. Unless he's a total idiot, and you can't be in this business, he already knows his first plan failed."

"Yeah, you're right." Gavin leaned against the hotel room desk. "I'm going to be at the funeral, of course. But do we want to go together or separately?"

"I don't think we have much choice since we both went to Johnny's office. His secretary saw us and might say something if we act like we don't know each other tomorrow."

"True."

Mick pounded his fist on his thigh in frustration, mixed he knew with anger at what had happened to Johnny.

"You have to stop thinking now," Gavin said, moving to Mick to grip his hand.

"Not happening," Mick muttered.

"Yeah, it is." Much to Mick's shock, Gavin kissed him.

"You have to unwind," Gavin said afterward, pulling away to look at him.

"That" — Mick rubbed his fingers over his lips — "was not the way to get me to... relax."

Gavin chuckled. "But what comes next should." He ran his hand over the front of Mick's jeans, squeezing his cock gently.

"Are you propositioning me?"

"Do I have to?"

"Hell, no!" Mick grabbed Gavin's shoulder, spinning him around to face the bed. "Undress now and get your ass on there."

"On my hands and knees?" Gavin replied, stripping quickly.

"Did I say that? This time you're going to be on your back, your legs pulled up as high as you can get them. Understand?" Mick slapped Gavin's ass to emphasize his order.

Gavin instantly obeyed, feeling more exposed and vulnerable than he ever had before with Mick. *But it's what he needs. What I need.* Mick brought his hand down hard on Gavin's butt—once, twice, and a third time, interrupting Gavin's thoughts. He cried out in pain.

"One more sound from you..." Mick growled. His eyes seemed to glitter in anticipation as he watched Gavin.

"Yes, Sir," Gavin whispered. That earned him two more slaps before Mick began to undress.

When Mick stood naked, he got the lube and a cock ring from his carry-on bag. After snapping the ring around the base of Gavin's throbbing member, Mick lubed two fingers and stabbed them into Gavin's waiting hole. "If you even think about making a noise..." he said as he began stroking Gavin's gland.

Gavin pressed his lips together but soon the pleasure flooding him became too much and he moaned. Mick brought his free hand down twice on Gavin's ass. "What did I tell you?"

Gavin almost didn't reply. Then he whispered, "To be..." He bit down hard to repress a cry when Mick smacked him one more time, the sound echoing through the room. Gavin was uncertain if he'd spoken to fulfill his own need for more punishment, or Mick's need to dole it out.

Pulling out his fingers, Mick quickly lubed his thick cock, pressed it against Gavin's entrance and thrust in, hard. As he did, he kept his gaze locked on Gavin's face. Much to Gavin's amazement, Mick paused, leaned forward and kissed him. He could smell Mick's sweat and the aroma of sex in the air. Both heated his need to the boiling point. Then Mick proceeded to fuck him into oblivion. At the last second, when Gavin thought he'd break again and beg for release, even if it earned him more punishment, Mick snapped the ring off and came with a shout of exultation. Gavin arched his body, his own orgasm consuming him.

"Holy fucking hell," Mick whispered several minutes later.

"Worked, didn't it?" Gavin said with a grin.

"Damned right it did. I feel like a wrung-out dishrag."

Gavin laughed. "Not a pretty description but I know what you mean."

"Now…" Mick sighed, "I suppose I have to move."

"Unless you want us glued together, it might be a good idea."

"Oh, we're full of sucky descriptions tonight."

"Speaking of which, that's one thing I didn't do. Suck you."

"Next time." Mick sighed, rolling off Gavin. "Shower?"

"Shower."

"Together?"

"Why the hell not? It saves…"

"If you say water…"

Gavin grinned. "Well it does." He bit back a groan as he eased off the bed. Not because his wounds hurt but his ass ached, inside and out. A pleasant ache, as far as he was concerned but still…

"Are you okay?" Mick asked with concern.

"Never better, other than I'm tired and sticky and *tired*," Gavin replied as he headed to the bathroom.

"Then we're in and out," Mick said, going past him to turn on the water.

"Been there, done that, about ten minutes ago, give or take."

Mick shook his head. "Gav, you are so asking for it."

"Not until morning, then we'll see."

After adjusting the water temperature, Mick stepped under the shower. Gavin quickly joined him and minutes later, washed and dried off, they crawled back into bed, clean but exhausted. Once more Mick surprised Gavin by kissing him quickly. Gavin returned it as given before Mick slung his arms around Gavin from behind, spooning against him, and they both fell asleep.

Chapter Ten

"Just like any other cemetery. Too many roads to figure out," Mick muttered as he and Gavin walked from the parking lot toward the section where they'd been told Johnny's funeral would be happening.

"Yeah," Gavin said tightly.

"Hey, are you okay?" From the dark expression Mick saw on Gavin's face, he wasn't certain Gavin was fine at all.

"Just remembering the last time I was in a graveyard. It was...when I buried Mira."

"Sorry," Mick said quietly. "If you want to..."

"I'll be fine. No way in hell am I going to back out just because of a memory." With a sharp nod, Gavin sped up, pointing to a small group of people several hundred yards ahead of them. "That must be where we're headed."

Mick knew it was when he saw Diana Walsh, Johnny's secretary—or ex secretary now, he supposed. He noted that she wore a dark skirt and blouse, as befitted a funeral, and that she was talking to a minister. "Guess she's in charge of things."

"Looks like," Gavin agreed. "With Johnny having no family…" He shrugged.

"And damned few friends from the look of it." Mick counted sixteen people, excluding himself and Gavin, most of them male. There were three women, each standing beside what he could only assume were their husbands.

Ms. Walsh glanced in Mick's direction, smiling sadly when she saw him. After saying something to the minister, she hurried over to Mick. "I'm so glad you came," she said by way of greeting.

"What else could I do? He was my friend." He shook his head. "From the turnout, I'm one of the very few he had."

"And half these people were his clients, not friends. I suppose I should be happy they cared enough to come say their goodbyes. I'll introduce you if you want. The service won't start for another ten minutes."

"That's okay. I'm sure you have other things you need to take care of." Mick smiled at her. "At least he had you to do this for him."

"Of course he did," she said, returning his smile with a small one of her own. "I ran the office and now…" Wiping away a tear, she hurried back to the minister.

Mick and Gavin moved closer to the grave site, both looking for tells that would let them know if any of the men present were the two they were searching for.

"Anything?" Mick asked Gavin under his breath.

"Possibly," Gavin replied just as quietly. "Look off to your left. There's someone standing in the shadows by that large elm tree."

All Mick could make out was that it was a man, maybe six foot in height, with dark hair. His face remained in shadow, probably on purpose.

"Could be one of us," Mick agreed as he went back to scanning the men closer to the grave site. "So could he," he murmured when his gaze met that of a stocky, muscular man who looked to be in his mid-thirties. "The guy in the blue shirt and dark slacks."

"Dead eyes," Gavin replied, smiling briefly.

"Definitely." Almost before the word was out of his mouth, the man in question strolled over to them.

"A friend of Morgan's, or just one of his clients?" the man asked.

"Old friend," Mick replied. "You?"

The man gave both Mick and Gavin a long, studied look before replying. "I worked for him a time or two. Tough way for him to die."

"Yeah."

"Had a bit of an...accident myself, day before yesterday, that almost ended the same way." The man smiled dryly. "Made me realize that my life is precious—at least to me."

"Know the feeling," Mick replied.

"I'm going to go check on something," Gavin said. "I'll be right back."

Mick nodded, suspecting Gavin was leaving so the man would feel more comfortable. Mick returned his attention to the man. "Seems to be a week for...accidents."

"You too?"

Mick nodded. "A lot of that going around, starting with Johnny."

"Who's your friend?" the man asked.

Mick raised an eyebrow. "Is it any of your business?"

"Maybe. Did he know Morgan too?"

"Nope."

A long pause followed as the man seemed to consider his next words. Then he said, "Name's Tom Jordan—for now."

"Good to meet you, Tom. I'm Rick." Mick smiled. "At least for now."

"That makes two of us."

"Maybe all three. Take a look at the guy over there." Mick barely nodded toward the elm tree.

"Yeah, I was thinking the same thing. Do we brace him?"

"Nah. Seems like he's the shy type."

Tom chuckled. "Aren't we all in some ways? Still, question is, is he number three or is he Morgan's killer?"

"Either or, though somehow I doubt he's the killer. No reason to think that. Just...instinct."

"I agree." Tom took out a pack of cigarettes and lighter. "Want one?" he asked.

"Nope. Not one of my vices," Mick replied as he watched Tom light up.

The man by the tree suddenly stepped into full view and walked slowly in their direction. He came to a stop a couple of yards away, eyeing them.

"Yes?" Mick said, eyeing him back.

"Just wondering something."

"Such as?" Tom asked.

The man paused then said, "Why the two of you keep looking at me."

"Trying to figure out if you're...to use his words—" Tom nodded at Mick, "number three."

"Three?"

"Never mind. Just a joke. Seems like most of the people here were only Johnny's clients. I was wondering if you were his third friend. If he even had that many."

"Guess you could call me that."

Rapping a knuckle on his teeth, Mick replied, "More of a long distance friend?"

"Yeah. You?"

Mick shrugged. "Friend of his, sort of, when I was younger. Then we went our separate ways. Ended up keeping in touch by email from time to time but that was it."

"So how did you find out about this?" The man looked pointedly at the grave site.

"Something happened I thought might interest him. Emailed him. No reply. Called. Got a 'this number is no longer in service'. So I came out here to find out why. Found out and wasn't happy."

"Same here, only I must have called earlier than you, Rick," Tom said. "I got hold of Ms. Walsh. She told me he'd been in a deadly accident."

"Accident my ass," the third man spat.

"Yeah, that's what we're figuring. You got a reason to feel the same?" Mick said.

"I'll tell you later. Looks like the funeral's starting. By the way, I'm Carl."

Tom chuckled. "At least for now?"

For a second Carl seemed puzzled. Then he nodded. "Yeah, for now."

The three men moved to stand beside the grave. Gavin came close, cocking his head at Mick in question. Mick nodded and Gavin joined them. Before Gavin could say anything, Mick quietly introduced him as Gary. Gavin obviously caught on, because he didn't look in the least surprised at his new name.

After that, the four men listened to the service. But Mick knew the others were wondering the same thing he was — was the killer there and watching them? — the person who had murdered Johnny and tried to have the three of them, including Carl, Mick suspected, killed as well.

* * * *

As Gavin and Mick headed back to the parking lot after the funeral, accompanied by the two other men, Gavin asked if any of them had gotten the feeling Johnny's killer had been at the grave site.

"If he was, you couldn't prove it by me," Carl said. "All I saw was a bunch of wishy-washy namby-pambies trying to look as if they cared about Johnny Morgan."

Gavin was tempted to tell Carl he was an ass. But given what the man did for a living, he kept his thoughts to himself.

Mick wasn't quite as polite about it. "Those people might not have known him well but he helped them out and they took the time and had the courtesy to come pay him their last respects."

"Okay, so maybe I was a bit out of line. It's been a rough couple of days."

"Yeah, you were going to tell us about that," Tom put in, eyeing him.

"I had a run-in with a cop who didn't like the fact I was trying to hold up a small town liquor store." Carl chuckled dryly. "Not my prime objective but the dude didn't know that. He walked in just as I was about to shoot the guy I was after. I was damned lucky someone came in right that second. The cop must have been a rookie 'cause he glanced at the old lady. Told her to get out. I'm the one who got out after shooting the cop."

Mick looked quickly at Gavin before asking Tom, "What kind of accident, as you put it, did you have?"

"Same song, different verse, and it wasn't really an accident. I just said that since I didn't know what was going on. I was supposed to make my target's death fit the bill for a double indemnity insurance claim."

"Me too," Carl put in.

"So anyway," Tom continued, "I did my research, had it all set up. The lady worked as a cashier at a gas station so I figured, since one of the reasons insurance companies pay double is murder by person or persons unknown, death during a holdup would fit the bill. Guess what happened when I walked in there."

"Cops showed up, just like with me and Carl there," Mick said, scowling.

"Got it in one, Rick. I managed to use the lady as a hostage to get out of there, dumped her body in an alley a few blocks away and beat it out of town."

"So we were all given the same kind of job," Mick said, as they got to his car. "I vote we meet somewhere less public and see if we can come up with who wants all of us out of business, starting with Johnny. From the sound of it he died right around the time all of us got the jobs."

"Hold that thought," Carl said. "And we can meet in my hotel room. I swept it, it's clear. Call me paranoid, but after I found out Johnny was dead, plus what happened to me, I wasn't about to take a chance someone might have followed me here, or figured I'd come down for Johnny's funeral."

"Same with me," Mick told him.

Gavin smiled to himself when Tom looked slightly nonplussed. *Apparently that isn't something the guy's used to doing. Probably figures since he travels alone it's not necessary. Stupid, if he makes any phone calls, but maybe he doesn't when he's in his room.*

"Toss you for which room we use," Carl said with a grin.

"Nah, I'm fine with yours. Give us the hotel and room number and we'll meet you there."

Carl told them, then the group split up, the other men heading for their rental cars.

"It could be one of them, you know," Gavin said as they pulled out of the cemetery parking lot.

Mick chuckled dryly. "I'm betting each of them is thinking the same thing." He drummed his fingers on the dashboard. "Could be, but I don't think so. Too bad shifters don't have mind reading abilities like vampires do."

"I do have the ability to sense people's emotions, although not as well in this form as when I'm a coyote. After all, coyotes are canines, just like wolves and dogs. If you ever had a dog as a pet, you'd know that he always seemed to know if you were happy or angry or sad even though you couldn't tell him you were in so many words."

"Never had a pet, but yeah, I've heard that about dogs. So, going with that idea, what did you sense about Tom and Carl?"

"I wasn't around them long enough but I do know they're both pissed as hell. But then they said as much. They're also very wary of me," Gavin added. "They can't figure out how I fit into things."

"It's none of their business."

"Mick," Gavin said, "if one of them had shown up with someone in tow, wouldn't you be wondering why? Presuming, of course, the person wasn't their wife."

"Yeah I guess so." Mick blew out a sharp breath.

"All we have to do when they ask, and they will, is tell them we work as a team. Sort of the, umm, Barney and Clyde of the hit man world."

Mick snorted out a laugh. "That works, although the name Barney reminds me of that TV show with the dumb deputy. Anyway, yeah, we'll tell them we're partners and leave it at that."

By then, they were driving past Carl's hotel.

"Find a place to park," Mick said, "but not too close. Then we'll go in through the service entrance. Better safe than sorry, since whoever's after us could have been at the funeral and would have seen all of us together."

"Agreed. Though how they'd know who we were..."

"They set up the three hits we were supposed to make and sent in the cops to stop us. It wouldn't surprise me if they were out there somewhere watching to be sure that their plan was working, even if it was at just one of the hits. Ergo, they'd know at least one of our faces."

"Good point." Gavin spotted a place to park a block past the hotel, pulled into it then, after feeding the meter enough for three hours, they headed to the back of the hotel hyper-aware of anyone who might show an untoward interest in them.

"We're good," Mick said when they reached the service entrance. Soon they were upstairs. He knocked on the door to Carl's room. The peephole darkened momentarily then Carl opened the door to let them in, putting the gun he held back in his waistband.

"Tom's not here yet?" Mick asked, glancing around the room, noting that the bathroom door stood open.

"Yeah, he's hiding in the closet, just in case you weren't you," Carl replied sarcastically.

"Okay, that was a dumb question, I guess."

"You want something to drink while we wait for him?"

"Water's fine for me. Gary?" Mick glanced at Gavin.

"Water too, thanks," Gavin said.

"I've got hard stuff, whiskey and vodka," Carl told them as he took two bottles of water from the small fridge by the sink.

Mick accepted the offered bottle. "We don't drink, other than a beer now and then for him."

Carl nodded. "Okay, question. You two work as a team?"

"Yep," Mick replied.

"Interesting. I've never tried that. Of course, first I'd have to find someone I trusted and in this business chances of that are slim to none."

"Rick and I got lucky with that," Gavin said, taking a deep drink of water.

Mick nodded, looking at the clock on the nightstand by one of the double beds. "What's taking Tom so long? He should have been here by now."

"Probably got caught in traffic," Carl replied, "or stopped to grab something to eat."

"Then he'd better bring some for us," Mick said with a small chuckle. "I'm starving."

"There's always room service." Carl grabbed the menu off the desk, handing it to Mick.

"Nah, I'll survive." Mick tossed the menu back on the desk on his way to the window. Pulling back the curtain, he looked down at the street in front of the hotel.

"So, Gary," Carl said, "tell me a bit about yourself. How'd you manage to hook up with Rick?"

Gavin grinned. "Would you believe it if I told you he was hired to kill me?"

"Not even. If he had been, you'd be dead, given his reputation."

"Maybe I was better than most people at keeping that from happening," Gavin replied, glancing quickly at Mick.

"What reputation?" Mick asked, his voice low and dangerous sounding.

Carl replied casually, "The one you must have or Johnny wouldn't have been using you. He only worked with the best. That's why there were only three of us."

Mick's response was just a sharp, "Okay, I guess I can accept that."

"Hey, you don't think I have anything to do with what happened, do you? Come on. I almost landed in jail. Would have if the old lady hadn't walked in at just the right second."

Since Carl was facing Mick at that moment, Gavin mouthed, "Truth," when Mick looked at him.

"Nah, Carl, I think we're all being targeted by someone who wants to put us out of business," Mick told him. "So ease it back a notch. Okay?"

"Yeah. Sorry. I'm just tense, which isn't good, all things considered. And damn it, where the hell is Tom?"

"Now *that* I can't answer," Mick said. "He should have been here by now."

"No kidding," Carl growled.

"Why don't I take a look around?" Gavin said. "You two can wait here in case he shows up. I know what he's driving, which will help."

"Ga—Gary. Not a smart idea," Mick told him, frowning.

"I'm not going to play hunting dog." Gavin winked at Mick. "I'll just do a walk through the place and around the outside, in case he got the room number wrong."

"Okay but don't make a day-long project out of it."

With a nod, Gavin left. After the door closed, Carl chuckled. "You almost blew it. Not that I thought his real name is Gary."

"Any more than yours is Carl, but we already know that."

"Yep." Carl wandered over to the window where Mick had been standing a few moments ago. After looking out, he turned back, a dry smile on his lips. "So what'll we do until Tom shows up or Gary comes back to tell us he's nowhere around? Tell war stories?"

"You can if you want. Me? I don't tell anyone what I do, or how I do it."

"Yeah, I was just joking." Carl eyed Mick. "You and Gary just business partners?"

"Yep. What? You thought we'd be more?"

Carl shrugged. "Happens sometimes. This is a solitary life. If you're not too particular and need someone to fuck to get rid of the stress…"

"I go find a prostitute," Mick replied. He decided to end that train of thought on Carl's part by turning on the TV. Going to an all-sports channel, he sat on the end of one of the beds to watch a game. Soon enough, Carl took a seat on the other bed and with a bit of prodding from Mick, they debated which team would win.

A knock on the door had both of them on instant alert. Mick indicated that Carl should answer, pulling out his gun to cover the man. Carl did as he had when Mick and Gavin had arrived, using the peephole to check who was there. Instantly Carl flew backward, a hole blossoming where his eye had been a second before.

Mick didn't bother to check to see if Carl was still alive. Instead, he dropped, crawling to the door. Reaching up, he unlocked it, flipped off the security latch and pulled it open. Jumping to his feet, he stood to one side, gripping his gun with both hands, waiting for the killer to enter. The sound of rapid footsteps receding down the carpeted hallway told him that wasn't happening but he still moved cautiously to see if he could catch a glimpse of the killer. All he saw was the door to the fire exit at the far end of the hall swinging closed. He knew that giving chase at that point would be an exercise in futility. All the person had to do was go up or down one flight into the next hallway and become just another hotel patron.

Besides which, Mick needed to wipe the room down to eliminate any of his or Gavin's fingerprints. He figured he had probably ten minutes at best before the cops showed up, since someone had to have heard the shot. He closed and locked the door again, stepped around Carl's body and began a methodical cleaning with a rag from the bathroom. Not that his prints were on file attached to his name, and he was fairly certain that Gavin's weren't either, but he wasn't about to take a chance. He removed the plastic liner from the wastebasket in the bathroom, dumped the menu, the two water bottles and the TV remote into it. They would go into a dumpster after he left the hotel.

"Need some help?"

Mick whirled around, bag in hand, to see Gavin standing there.

"We might want to hurry. Three cop cars pulled up in front of the hotel a minute ago. It won't take them long to get up here. I take it" — Gavin toed Carl's corpse — "this wasn't your doing." He gripped Mick's arm and instantly transported them to their own hotel room.

"Nope, it wasn't," Mick answered the moment they'd landed then told him what had happened.

"Chalk that up to another way to eliminate someone," Gavin said.

Mick chuckled low. "Been there, done that. You'd have thought Carl would have known better. Guess he didn't. Any sign of Tom?"

"Not ace-deuce. No him, no car. That sort of eliminates him as Carl's killer."

"Or not, if he was smart enough to leave the car somewhere and walk or cab it over here," Mick pointed out.

"If he did, I wasn't on the spot to see him come inside."

"Well, you couldn't be everywhere at once."

"Yeah. Still..." Gavin sighed, dropping onto the bed. "You know, it almost had to be him. He's the only other person beside us who knew where Carl was staying."

"In theory," Mick replied, "but who knows how careful Carl was about coming back here. Hell, we took precautions but a good tracker could have followed us as well. At least to the hotel. Getting his room number would only mean knowing what name he used to sign in. Or..." Mick frowned. "Or our friendly killer used a small parabolic listening device at the cemetery. That's where we were when Carl gave us the information."

"Possible. Either way, he found him and if Tom wasn't the shooter, he might have become a victim as well. I suggest we pack up and move to somewhere safer."

"Just where would that be?" Mick asked.

"Get online and find a realty site. Pick an available house that's been on the market for a while. Preferably one without neighbors cheek by jowl to it. I'll pack our stuff."

"Clever. Something you've done before, I take it." Mick said, getting an affirmative nod from Gavin. He did as Gavin suggested and soon had three places to choose from.

"That one," Gavin said, reaching over his shoulder to tap the screen.

"It's boarded up and there are no walls, just framework on the ground floor," Mick muttered.

Gavin pointed to the information. "It was being remodeled when the owner went bankrupt and decided to put it on the market. It's not a place that's going to get tons of people wanting to look at it. Besides which, it's not as if we're going to take up residence. We just need a safe place to crash for a few days until we track down the person who at this point probably has their sights set on you as the last of Johnny's crew."

"Yeah, good point." Mick scrolled through the rest of the pictures so Gavin could choose a landing spot. Then he shut down, putting the laptop in the bag with his weapons. Getting his other bag, he slung both over his shoulder while Gavin did the same with his carry-on bag. Then Gavin teleported them to the attic of the house.

Enough late-afternoon sun shone through the small, unwashed windows to let them move about without stumbling over anything. They did a bit of exploring and found a couple of mattresses, covered with plastic, stashed at the far end of the attic.

"Home sweet home," Gavin said, laughing, as they moved the mattresses to an open area and laid them down.

Mick snorted, suggesting they go downstairs to see if the water was still turned on. "Not that I'm planning on taking a shower, mind you," he said. "But bathroom facilities would be nice."

Luckily there was running water and the toilet worked too, even though the bathroom itself could have used a good cleaning.

"It's no worse than one in the nearest gas station," Gavin pointed out.

After settling in as much as possible, all things considered, Mick sat on the mattresses and flipped open his laptop. When Gavin asked how he could get online, Mick told him that he could pirate anyone's wireless service in the area, secure or not, and went on to prove his point.

"What are you looking for?"

"Ms. Walsh's address," Mick replied as he did a search. "It occurred to me we can't eliminate her, either, as the shooter or working with someone else who did the actual killing."

"Good point, if she knew more about what Johnny did than she let on."

"Well now," Mick murmured when he found her residence. "Our lowly secretary lives in a high-rent district if the address she gave the officials at the cemetery is correct."

"Boy, I'll say," Gavin commented when Mick flicked through the pictures on the rental site for her building. "You hacked into the cemetery files?" When Mick nodded, Gavin patted his shoulder, muttering, "You have hidden talents. If that is her real address, she either inherited a lot of money or she was more than just his secretary."

"Or she has a wealthy lover." Mick nodded thoughtfully. "I wonder…"

"Is there a way to find out how long she's been living there?"

"I can try." A couple of minutes later, Mick said, "Six months."

"Interesting."

"No shit."

"Is she the only one on the lease?"

"Yep."

Gavin paced, thinking. "Surveillance time."

"Works for me but from where? Her place is on the fifteenth floor."

"Show me the Earth View of her building."

Mick brought it up and Gavin sat beside him to see what was around the building. "Do you know which windows are hers?"

It took Mick a minute, and the apartment building site's information page, but he found the answer to Gavin's question.

"Good," Gavin said. "We can start here." He indicated which building he meant then got up to get their binoculars out of Mick's weaponry bag while Mick shut down his laptop.

"Gotta love Air Coyote," Mick said seconds later when they landed on the rooftop.

"It's the 'ooonly way to fly', to quote a now defunct airline's slogan."

"Better believe it," Mick replied as he moved to the edge of the roof. Lying on his stomach to keep the lowest profile possible, he took the binoculars Gavin handed to him and began studying the windows of Ms. Walsh's apartment. Gavin joined him, doing the same thing. The sun lowered to the west of them, silhouetting the building. The only light burning in the apartment came from the front entryway that Mick could barely make out across the depth of the living room.

"Looks like she's not home," Mick told Gavin.

"Want me to do some recon?"

Mick rapped a fingernail on the binoculars. "You can do it in the dark. Right?"

"If you mean, do I have good night vision, it's better than a normal human's but not spectacular."

"Better works. Just go through the place to see if it looks like she's sharing it with someone."

"Got it." Gavin vanished.

Seconds later, Mick saw him in Ms. Walsh's living room. "I feel like the guy in that movie," he muttered as he tried to follow Gavin's movements through the rest of the apartment, picking up on his shadow a time or two, caused by the ambient city light going through the windows.

"She definitely has a roommate," Gavin said, reappearing beside Mick. "Or at least a man who spends enough time there to have clothes in one of the bedroom closets."

"Now all we have to do is find out who he is. Of course, this might all be a wild goose chase but…"

"But she *is* hiding something. When she told us about her—how did she put it? Her casual relationship with Johnny? Yeah, that was it. I thought she was just embarrassed about admitting it. The whole boss–secretary cliché. Then at the funeral, her grief seemed…forced. Like she knew it was what was expected of her."

Mick scowled. "Why the hell didn't you say something before now?"

"Because she was never on our radar until an hour ago, so it didn't really seem important."

"Damn it, Gav, you should know that every detail is important. Both from what you used to do and from what we do now." Mick thought back to the funeral, trying to remember if the woman had seemed to be interested in, or avoiding looking at, any of the men there. As far as he could recall, she hadn't done either. Her attention had been on the minister and talking to the few people in attendance with no undertones that any of them was more than they seemed.

"Sorry," Gavin said contritely.

"Did you pick up on anything else in there?"

"Yes. I know the man's scent. It's not one we've run into before."

"Okay. That eliminates Tom. At least as her partner if she's behind all this."

"It doesn't eliminate him as the killer, though, since we still don't know if he's dead or in the wind."

"True."

After that, Gavin and Mick settled in behind the parapet, not talking as they waited for Ms. Walsh to return home. That didn't happen until much later in the evening. When she arrived, a man accompanied her, whose presence shocked the hell out of Mick.

Chapter Eleven

When the door to Ms. Walsh's apartment opened and she walked into the entryway, Gavin saw the figure of a man just behind her. He didn't recognize him, but it was very apparent from the stream of swearwords coming from Mick that his friend did. And that Mick was not happy—not in the least.

"Okay, mind telling me who that is?" Gavin asked.

"A man who is supposed to be dead. No wonder it was a graveside funeral and there was no viewing of the body."

Gavin caught on instantly. "Johnny Morgan."

"In the flesh. What the hell is going on here? Who the hell was killed by the hit-and-run driver and why didn't the cops know it wasn't him?"

"We need to find out who identified the body, although I suspect we know at this point. Obviously, whoever the man was, he was carrying Johnny's ID and he must have at least had some resemblance to Johnny. If Ms. Walsh was the one who said the victim was him, the cops would have had no reason to doubt her."

"No shit. But why? I mean, why is he trying to get rid of us? Of me and Carl and Tom? We made him a small fortune, to put it mildly."

"Maybe Ms. Sweetheart there didn't like how he made his primary income."

"But that's none of her damned business."

Gavin looked at him as if he was unbelievably naïve "Have you ever known a man who didn't think with his dick when it came to keeping a woman around that he wanted? If she laid down the law, told him to quit what he was doing and get rid of the—well, evidence I suppose, meaning the three of you—and he's into her enough that he doesn't want to lose her…"

"No wonder I don't like women," Mick muttered. "Sneaky, conniving bitches."

"Not all of them are that bad," Gavin responded with a small smile. "Besides which, he didn't have to go along with her."

"Like you said, he was thinking with his dick, if we're right about this. Or… She's the one who's doing the killing and he doesn't know what's going on."

"How do you explain the fact he's still alive and kicking if that's the case?" Gavin asked him. "And went along with her plan to pretend that he was dead? Because obviously he had to."

"She… Hell, I don't know, Gav. I just can't believe he would try to take me out. We've been friends since we first met, damn it. That's been over six years now."

"How often in all that time have you actually been in contact with him when it didn't involve a job? When it did, your only interaction was through email. Right?"

Mick nodded. "And that was hardly contact in the real sense of the word. Just 'Here's what the client needs' and 'Here's the information on the target' from him, and my price for doing it, minus his cut."

"So after you agreed to work for him, that was the last time the two of you actually met face to face?"

"Well… Yeah. It was safer that way."

"Damn it, Mick, that's not friendship. That's a business arrangement, pure and simple." It was only friendship in his mind, because Mick had needed someone, anyone whom he could call a friend and Johnny was the only person who had fit the bill. Gavin wanted to hold him. To tell him he had a real friend now, in every sense of the word. *No, more than a just a friend. Someone – me – who would do anything to keep him safe and…and try to make him truly happy for once in his life. But this is not the time or place.* He smiled wryly, looking around the rooftop. *Definitely not the place.*

"I know that," Mick said tightly, scrubbing his hand through his hair. He looked across at Ms. Walsh's windows. "Now I *really* know it, I guess." Mick moved away from the edge of the roof and stood. "Let's get back to our hideout and decide what to do next."

As soon as they landed in the attic of the house, Mick started toward his laptop. Gavin stopped him with two words.

"Come here." When Mick turned, Gavin held out his arms. "Come here. Please?"

"If you think us fucking is going to make…make his betrayal less painful…"

"It won't. But it might help you realize you have someone who really is your friend – and more, if only you'd admit it. I hope you know that already. Someone who will give you what you need without expecting anything in return."

Mick seemed almost bashful as he moved into Gavin's arms. "I've sort of figured that out, even though I have trouble believing it at times." Then he lifted an eyebrow. "You don't get anything in return when we fuck?"

"Yeah, a sore ass. Not that I'm complaining."

"If we do it now, you have to…"

"Obey your orders. Don't you think I've learned that by this time?"

Mick untangled himself from Gavin's embrace. "You have. But… Things have changed now. So I need to know, is it what you *want*?"

Gavin gave that serious thought before replying. "Yes. Not as punishment, because I don't feel guilty for what happened to Mira. Not anymore. And not because I know you need to inflict pain on me because I'm here and whoever you're pissed at isn't."

"Isn't that why you're offering now? To be…a stand-in for Johnny?" Mick frowned then chuckled. "Okay, that didn't quite come out the way I meant it."

"I would hope not," Gavin said with a small laugh. "To answer your question—no. Well, not entirely. As I said, you need to understand that I'm willing to be your friend and lover on all levels, no matter what. Fucking is one of the most intimate ways of proving it. At least as I see it."

"Yes, I suppose it is. I never really thought about it that way. Probably because I never had someone in my life who…who gave a damn about me."

"Well, you do now. So…?"

Mick hesitated then came close enough to kiss him quickly before saying with a wicked smile, "Strip. Now."

"No, you first. I promised you the next time we did this I was going to suck you."

"Are you trying to tell me what to do?"

"No, Sir," Gavin replied, falling into his role. "I was just reminding you…" He lowered his gaze, letting it linger on Mick's crotch.

"Strip—me," Mick ordered.

"With pleasure, Sir." He pulled Mick's T-shirt off him in one swift move. Then, kneeling, he slowly undid the button on Mick's jeans and provocatively pulled down the zipper before inching the tight denim fabric over Mick's hips until the jeans slid down to pool around his feet. Taking Mick's hardening cock in his hand, Gavin teased his tongue up the length, lapping the sensitive slit, before drawing the pulsing head into his mouth.

"Shi-it," Mick moaned, thrusting forward.

Gavin took him in all the way, swallowing hard around Mick's now thoroughly engorged member. As Gavin worked his magic, Mick dug his nails into Gavin's shoulders. Gavin relished the pain, as minor as it was in the grand scheme of what he knew would follow.

Suddenly Mick pulled out, growling, "I know what you're trying to do. On there, face down, ass in the air, now!"

Mick pointed to the mattresses and Gavin complied instantly.

Two sharp slaps to his ass had Gavin fisting his hands but he refused to cry out. Two more followed and he bit back a deep groan—one that would have been a mixture of need and pain.

"You are not to come until I tell you that you can. Is that understood?"

"Yes, Sir," Gavin whispered.

"Speaking?" Mick slapped Gavin's ass again. "You know the rules."

Gavin nodded rapidly in reply. There was a momentary pause, then three lubed fingers pushed through his tight ring of muscle. Mick began stroking Gavin's gland, delivering a hard blow to his ass when Gavin involuntarily moaned from the pleasure the action invoked.

Mick pulled his fingers out. Gavin closed his eyes — waiting. Within seconds, Mick's hard cock had filled Gavin so hard and fast he couldn't suppress a cry of pain. He knew what would follow and his muscles tightened anticipating the expected slaps.

Instead, Mick leaned down, murmuring, "It will be all right." Then he followed his surprising words with, "Remember, you don't come until I tell you to."

Gavin found out that was much easier said than done. It took more willpower than he'd thought he possessed not to explode as Mick rode him hard and fast. Just when he was certain he couldn't take one second more of the pure ecstasy Mick was giving him, his lover came with a shout of elation, followed quickly by a gasped out "Now" as Mick collapsed, shaking, on Gavin's back.

Gavin responded with a jubilant cry of his own, trembling from head to toe with the strength of his orgasm. Then he too collapsed and they ended up in a pile on the mattresses.

"That was...as always with you...perfect," Mick murmured, the words punctuated by short pants as he regained his breath.

"I could try to be witty and say in that case I guess we don't have to do it again."

"Get that thought out of your head right now."

Gavin laughed. "It's already just a memory."

"Good."

Mick started to sit up but Gavin wasn't having any of that.

"Now we sleep, like it or not. There's not a damned thing we can do tonight that won't be better accomplished when we aren't brain dead."

"True, I suppose. Do you mind if I at least hit the bathroom and wash up first?"

"No. I'll be right behind you."

Mick snorted out a laugh. "That, my man, is my position."

"How can you be behind you?" Gavin asked with feigned, wide-eyed innocence.

"Damn, Gav." Mick laughed and got up. "You're good for me. In case I haven't said it before."

"And vice versa," Gavin replied softly. "Very much so."

Chapter Twelve

"The first thing we need to do is figure out whose idea it was to eliminate you and the others," Gavin said early the next morning after he and Mick had dressed.

"Yeah, and that ain't going to be easy. It's not like we can just walk up to Ms. Walsh and ask her. Well... We could. But good luck in getting her to admit Johnny's even alive, never mind her telling us where he's hiding out."

"You don't think it's at her place?"

"No. Yeah, he was there last night. And yeah, those are undoubtedly his clothes you saw there. But he'd be a fool to live with her where he could be spotted coming and going. Best bet is she snuck him in last night for a bit of hanky-panky."

Gavin chuckled. "Hanky-panky?"

Mick just scowled at him and began pacing the attic. "He wouldn't be at his home either."

"Do you know where that is?"

"I know where it was when we first met." Mick shrugged. "Since then, I'm sure he upgraded with all the money he was making off of us. I suppose we should check it out anyway, just in case."

"Get your laptop and bring the address up on the map program, in Earth View."

When Mick did, Gavin studied the area, telling Mick he was looking for a good place to land where his arrival wouldn't be seen. As he did, he commented, "Not exactly a mansion."

"No kidding. But at that point, he was just a P.I. Hell, he still is, as far as his cover goes. Well, was anyway until all this started to go down."

"Okay. I'll be back in a couple."

"Not taking me with you?"

"We just need to know if he's still living there. That doesn't take the two of us."

"True," Mick said to empty air when Gavin vanished. Since he had his laptop open anyway, he decided to try something. Going to the email account he used for communicating with Johnny, he composed a carefully worded letter, directed to Ms. Walsh, asking if she was keeping Johnny's 'other business' open even though she'd closed down the office. 'If so, you know how to get in contact with me,' he said at the end. After encrypting it, he sent it off through the usual secure channels and deleted the original.

Now to see if she, or Johnny, is still tracking that account.

He looked up when he caught movement out of the corner of his eye, going for the gun at the small of his back.

"If you shoot me, go for my heart or it won't do you any good," Gavin said with a low laugh. "He's not living there now. Hasn't been for five years, according to a very nice and very nosy neighbor lady who I talked to."

After holstering his gun again, Mick told Gavin what he'd done. "I doubt I'll get a reply but who knows? She might use it as a way to draw me out into the open so she or Johnny can try again to eliminate me."

"At any point, did you tell Johnny that the two of us were working together?" Gavin asked.

"Nope. Figured that was none of his business. Of course, Ms. Walsh has seen us together but for all she knows you're just a friend I'm staying with while I'm in town."

"That works. And he doesn't know where you live?"

"No. I told you it's… It was my safe place where I could get away from everything."

"Obviously he has no clue about the condo," Gavin said thoughtfully.

"What are you thinking? Because, if it has anything to do with our leaving town, forget it. I want the two of them dead and gone."

Before Gavin could reply, a ding indicated that Mick had email. He opened it, smiling tightly at the reply before showing it to Gavin.

"Does she…? Do they really expect you to fall for that?" Gavin asked.

Mick shrugged. "I'd say so. Using Johnny's old office is clever on her part. It's a place I know, so it would make sense that she'd choose it for our meeting. At that hour of night, the only people around will probably be security guards." Mick smiled dryly. "She's counting on me to be stupid enough to just walk right into whatever trap she has in mind."

"Since she doesn't know that you know Johnny's still alive, it works for what they're undoubtedly planning."

"True. If she and Johnny really are in this together."

"Mick," Gavin said firmly, "you know they have to be. As much as it hurts on some level, because you thought of him as a friend, she couldn't have pulled off his 'death' without him being complicit in the con."

"It is a con, isn't it? At least on some level."

"Absolutely," Gavin replied. "And it might have worked if they hadn't shown up together at her apartment last night while we were watching."

"Yeah." Mick reread the email, shaking his head, then shredded it before closing down the laptop. "Let's get breakfast then go over there. I may decide to go in before she expects me to. That'll give me the upper hand. If so, I have to figure out how to get inside when the time comes."

"Why don't we just teleport in?"

"She's going to expect me to do it her way. Meet her in the lobby." Mick chuckled. "If I do, then you'll teleport in and wait. Another reason to look around — to find a safe place for you to do that. My bet is that they're going to try to take me out and claim I was breaking into the building or his office. If I decide to go in before she's expecting me, then yeah, you can teleport both of us in."

"Makes sense to me. So let's go find somewhere with decent food, a near-new shop for something to wear over what we have on, then reconnoiter."

* * * *

Once they were well away from Johnny's building, after their recon mission, Mick and Gavin went into a fast-food restaurant's washroom. They took off the hoodies and caps they wore as well as the loose-fitting camo pants they had on over their jeans, then put the things in the shopping bag Mick had stashed in one pocket of the camos for just that purpose.

"Well, that killed three hours. Now what?" Mick said when they were back on the street.

"Now we see the sights."

"You are so kidding. We play tourist?"

Gavin grinned. "You have a better idea that doesn't involve sex?"

"Well, no."

"Good. So where to? The aquarium? The Field Museum? The Sky Deck?"

"The what?" Mick asked, bemused.

"The Sky Deck. I guess you can see the whole city from there."

"Umm, sure. Why not?"

Later, Mick pointed out the buildings he knew to Gavin. "This is almost as good as the view from the top of the Empire State Building."

"You can see all of Chicago from there?" Gavin asked with a wide grin.

Mick laughed. "Maybe on a really clear day, with high-power binoculars and a good imagination?"

They stayed there for close to an hour before deciding to move on to one of the city's many museums. It wasn't until they were inside the museum that Mick had the feeling they had been followed. How, he had no idea.

"Unless one of them spotted us checking out Johnny's building," Gavin said when Mick told him as soon as they were away from the tourist crowds.

"Possible, despite the fact we were real careful, both there and when we left the restaurant after getting rid of what we were wearing."

"They know your face, Mick. And Ms. Walsh knows mine."

"So do I."

Mick and Gavin whirled around to see who had spoken. Tom leaned against the wall, eyeing them. "Surprise," he said with an ironic smile.

"Hell, man, we figured you for dead and gone, so yeah, it is."

"Like Carl?"

"You know about that?"

"Yep. Someone came after me first, after all of us left the cemetery." He paused then said, pointing to a bench well away from the few people in the room, "Let's take this somewhere a bit more private."

"So, as I was saying," Tom continued quietly once the three men were seated. "I was halfway to the hotel on the Dan Ryan, when a car cut me off. I figured it was just some idiot who didn't know how to drive, so I started to go around him. I heard a shot and my tire blew. Whoever fired the shot waited until just the right second. They sped up, while I damn near went into the wall trying to get control of the car. Barely missed getting creamed by a semi in the process. And I mean it was so close I could have stepped into the cab if I'd had a mind to without opening my car door. Once I stopped shaking, I made it off the expressway. Left the car… It was a rental so" — he shrugged — "and grabbed a taxi. Had it drop me off three blocks from the hotel. I was about to go inside when the cops showed up. I figured the only reason they were there was because something had gone down and either you" — he looked at Mick — "or Carl was dead or dying, so I got out of there. I've been lying low ever since."

"How did you find me?" Mick asked sharply. "Wait, we'll get to that later." He looked past Tom at Gavin, who sat on the other side of Tom. "It must have been both of them, given the timing."

"My thought exactly," Gavin agreed.

"Both of who? And I found you just by damned luck. I was going stir-crazy, decided to go find something to eat. Imagine my surprise when I saw the two of you coming out of the Willis Tower. I got lucky, managed to flag down a taxi and had him follow you." Tom chuckled. "Shades of a bad movie. Anyway, when you ended up here… Well, here I am too."

Again, Mick glanced at Gavin, who nodded, mouthing, "True."

So Mick answered Tom's question. "Both are Ms. Walsh, who you saw at the funeral, and Johnny Morgan."

"The hell you say!"

"We were debating if both of them were involved or if Johnny was just her patsy, or vice versa. But one person probably couldn't have tried to get you killed, then have shown up at the hotel in time to shoot Carl unless they timed it down to the second. So they have to be working together."

"But why?" Tom asked.

"Something we'd like to know too," Gavin replied.

Tom looked between them. "I asked at the funeral and you put me off, but what's his"—he nodded toward Gavin—"connection to all this. As far as I know, Johnny only had three of us working for him."

"Gary's a friend of mine. We grew up together and he knows more about me than anyone else in the world, bar none," Mick replied before Gavin could.

"Okay, that works. If you trust him, I guess I do too. So… What are we going to do about Johnny and his lady friend?"

"Take them down," Mick told him. "I have an appointment to meet her tonight at Johnny's old office."

Tom looked at Mick as if he was crazy. "You know it's got to be a setup, especially if they're both in this together."

"No shit."

"You want more backup?"

"More?"

"Well, I was figuring Gary here was going along."

"He's not. He may know about me, but this is not something he'd be good at," Mick replied.

"Yeah, me and guns are not on speaking terms," Gavin said.

Mick grinned. "He's more into 'make love, not war'."

"I...see." Tom shrugged. "Not my thing but to each their own."

"Exactly," Mick said gruffly. "Okay, before we go any further, let's find a much less public place to talk. Like in the car, down by the lake."

Tom didn't look as if he liked that idea in the least. It didn't take Mick but a second to figure out why. "Look, if we wanted you dead, you'd already be a corpse in the men's room over there. So either you trust us or you can go on your way and I'll deal with this alone."

"No, I want in. Let's get out of here."

The drive to the lake shore passed in tense silence. Enough so that when Gavin found a parking place, he suggested they get out and walk. His two companions balked at first then agreed it might not be such a bad idea after all when Gavin pointed out the fresh air and late afternoon sunshine might help them relax. When

Mick snickered softly, Gavin shot him a smile of amusement but refrained from commenting.

"All right, what's the layout?" Tom asked when they reached the edge of the lake. "I've never been to Johnny's office."

"The building's an older one and sits on a corner. Retail on the ground floor. Main entrance to the lobby on the east side," Mick rattled off. "Elevators opposite the entrance. Security-info desk between them. Johnny's office is on the fifth floor with windows that are on the back side of the building, facing an alley. When you get off the elevator, there's a hall going right and left, and one straight ahead. The single corridor leads to a second hall paralleling the first one and past it to the back of the building."

Tom nodded, closing his eyes. Mick figured he was visualizing what he'd been told.

"What other access points are there to the building?" Tom asked.

Picking up a thin piece of driftwood, Mick made a quick sketch in the sand. "Service entrance off the alley, here" — he pointed — "and another one on the fourth side that doesn't face either street. Walkway between that side and the adjacent building."

"Roof entrance?" Tom asked.

"Two. Secured. Also two fire escapes, one each on the non-street facing sides of the building. One for the hall next to the elevators, the other you get to at the end of the hall heading to the back of the building. All entrances are alarmed — fire escape and rooftop."

"Got it. I assume Ms. Walsh is going to meet you in the lobby, since she's expecting you?"

"Yep." Mick didn't mention what had been his alternate plan. Now that Tom was involved, Mick didn't see a need to get into the building without Ms. Walsh knowing he had.

"Good. That'll give me a chance to get to Morgan's office while she's downstairs."

"Yep. Your best bet is the service entrance off the alley and use the stairs to get up to the fifth floor."

"I disagree," Gavin said. "The back fire escape would be better."

"How do you figure?" Mick asked. "I just said all the doors are alarmed."

"That's why we go back to the building now, while we can get into it since it's still office hours. Disarm the alarm on the fifth floor and you'll be set. Tom goes in that way. It puts him on the spot with less chance of the security guards seeing him."

Mick nodded, looking at Tom. "That work for you?"

"Does. Also gives me a chance to see the place first-hand."

"Yep. We have clothes in the trunk of the car we used when we reconnoitered this morning. You can use Gavin's. He'll wait in the car while we go inside."

They did as Mick said, he and Tom putting on the clothing Mick and Gavin had used earlier in the day over what they were wearing. While Gavin waited in a parking lot a block from the building, Tom and Mick went inside. When they got to the fifth floor, Mick walked Tom down to the rear hallway, pointing out Johnny's office from where they stood before going to the fire escape door.

With the tools Mick always carried with him when on a job, he easily disarmed the alarm. As they started to return to the elevator, they heard footsteps approaching from the direction of Johnny's office. Mick pointed to a door marked 'Janitor' and they quickly entered what turned out to be a supply closet.

Leaving the door open a crack, Mick watched as someone, he guessed from one of the other offices, walked down to the elevators. When they were gone, he and Tom went back downstairs, left the building and rejoined Gavin at the car.

"Mission accomplished?" Gavin asked.

"Yep," Mick replied. "Now I suggest we split up until tonight. She's expecting me at ten so she'll be in the lobby at that point. Tom, you could probably hide…"

"In that janitor's closet. At least until I hear the two of you going to the office."

"I'll make sure to talk to her when we get off the elevator to clue you in."

"That works."

"Once she and I are in the office, wait outside it."

"I have a bionic ear I'll bring with me. As soon as I know Morgan's there, I'll join you."

"How about we use a code word instead, just in case she's planned this on her own. Unlikely, but…"

"Okay. You have one in mind?"

Mick thought for a moment then nodded. "City boy. Gary called me that once and I guess it fits, and it's easy enough to work into a conversation if she's got a gun pointed at me."

Gavin chuckled. "Rick is definitely more city than country."

"Anything else you need from me before I split?" Tom asked.

"Nope. Just remember to bring a couple of weapons with you." Mick grinned when Tom rolled his eyes before taking off.

"I think he's good people," Mick said when he got into the car.

"Considering what he does for a living. Yeah," Gavin agreed. "Just like you."

Mick smiled, patting Gavin's thigh. "Considering what I do for a living?"

"Well, I'm hardly an innocent bystander anymore, when it comes down to it." Gavin turned the key in the ignition then pulled out of the lot.

"Gav," Mick replied with a grin, "You haven't been innocent since the first night I met you. And that has nothing to do with our job."

"Speaking of which, what happens now as far as that goes? With Johnny out of the picture—or he soon will be—we'll need to find someone to replace him."

"True. I might know someone who can help us with that. But we'll worry about it after we take care of Johnny and Ms. Walsh."

* * * *

"Good evening, Mick. I'm glad you showed up," Ms. Walsh said after she unlocked the lobby door to let him in.

Mick smiled dryly. "I never turn down an invitation from a pretty lady."

She arched an eyebrow at that but didn't respond. Instead, she said, "I'll tell you why I wanted to meet you once we're upstairs." She led the way to the elevator and as soon as they were in it and the door had closed she added, "If you don't mind I'd like to search you for weapons."

"Feel free to, as I'm not carrying." That was the truth, so far as it went. He had no weapons on him, having known this was likely to happen, but he'd be armed once he picked up the knife Gavin would have already stashed for him on top of the fire hose box across from the elevators on the fifth floor. In an amateur's hands, it wouldn't have been much defense against an armed attacker. In his hands... "Well, experience makes all the difference," he'd explained when Gavin had been doubtful about its usefulness.

She ran her hands over him, looking slightly surprised when she found out he'd been telling the truth. When they reached the fifth floor, she started down the hallway Johnny's office, obviously expecting him to follow. He did, pausing just long enough to retrieve the knife in its sheath and clip it to his belt at the small of his back.

When they got to the office, Ms. Walsh unlocked the door and stepped aside to let Mick enter. He feigned deep shock when he saw Johnny leaning casually against the receptionist's desk.

"What the hell!" Mick spat out loudly enough so that Tom could hear him.

"Surprised?" Johnny's smile was almost gleeful.

"Fuck yeah. I was at your damned funeral. What's the hell is going on here?"

"Have a seat and we'll explain," Johnny replied before casting a questioning glance at Ms. Walsh.

"He's clean," she told him, closing the door before crossing to sit in the chair behind the desk. Opening a drawer, she pulled out a pistol, pointing it at Mick. "Please do as he said." She waved it toward one of the client's chairs along the side wall.

Grimly, Mick obeyed. "I guess this isn't going to end pleasantly for me. Why, Johnny? Why kill Carl—or whatever his real name was—and probably Tom as well?"

"Necessity. Diana and I have plans and they don't include keeping that end of my business going. However, as she pointed out, the three of you knew too much about me, especially you. We couldn't start our new life knowing that at any time you might show up. Or, worse yet, let the authorities know about me and thus put me and my past clients in danger if the Feds accessed my accounts."

Mick snorted. "If we did that we'd be putting ourselves in the bull's-eye too."

"I'm sure you'd have figured out a way to keep that from happening. Be that as it may, it's not going to be an option."

"Why let me know you're still alive?"

Johnny shrugged. "For old time's sake. Unlike the other two, you and I were friends of a sort. I wanted, as corny as it sounds, to say goodbye."

"A friend who did his best to get me arrested, or worse, on the last job you sent my way."

Johnny frowned. "The last job I gave you was the one to take out the client's gold-digging wife and her boyfriend. I don't see how that would have brought in the cops unless you got really careless. That wouldn't have been like you."

"You seem to have forgotten the one for the client who wanted the target killed in such a way that he or she could have invoked the double indemnity clause of an insurance claim. The same kind of jobs you sent Carl and Tom on."

"No fucking way!" Johnny spat.

Both men immediately turned their attention to Ms. Walsh. She grinned wickedly. "I figured if I could get the three of you out of our hair that way, it would make things so much easier."

"But you didn't..." Johnny started to say.

"Know how you worked things? Of course I did. I'm not as stupid as you take me for." She smiled, still keeping the gun trained on Mick. "With them gone, I could start blackmailing your past clients and there would be no one to stop us. I saved all the information before you deleted it."

"You what?" Johnny looked at her in horror. "I thought... What about our plans? A home, living the good life?"

"Just how were we going to finance it? You spent money as fast as you made it." She shot a glance at Mick. "Your boss here might have been smart about setting everything up but when the money rolled in, most of it went up his nose or was gambled away. Saving was not a word in his vocabulary."

Mick shook his head. "You are unbelievable, Ms. Walsh. No wonder women aren't my thing. You can't trust them any further than you can throw them."

She smiled almost playfully, waving her gun between Johnny and Mick. "Luckily for me, neither of you will have to worry about women or anything else real soon."

"Shoot him, I take you out," Mick said quietly. "Shoot me... Well, hopefully he's got whatever it takes to deal with you before you manage to shoot him. Us city boys are good about that."

Even before the last words were out of his mouth, Mick pulled his knife, leaping to one side when she shot. The door to the office flew open and Tom appeared, while Gavin stepped into the room from what had been Johnny's office. Gavin gripped Johnny's arm and twisted it behind his back, forcing him to the floor beside Ms. Walsh. Then he put one foot on the small of Johnny's back to keep him there.

At the same time, Tom fired, winging Ms. Walsh when she aimed her gun at him. She cried out in pain and Mick took advantage of the chaos to swiftly grab her from behind and draw the knife across her throat.

Blood spurted, most of it hitting Johnny as he lay on the floor at her feet.

"Don't kill me," Johnny pleaded, looking up at Mick. "I didn't know. I swear. I just... I went along with her idea about my seeming death but that was it."

"That makes you complicit in the death of an innocent man," Mick replied coldly.

"He was just a bum we found on the street."

"And he deserved to die because of that? Him, and Carl? All so you could live happily ever after with...that." He pointed to Ms. Walsh's body. "You knew she planned on killing me. You said so yourself. You were here because you wanted to 'say goodbye' before she did."

"No, I swear—"

"You're a fucking liar. You might not have known about her blackmail plans, but twenty to one says you knew she was responsible for killing Carl and for the attempt on Tom's life." Glancing at Tom, Mick said, "Give me your gun, or take care of him yourself. Makes no never mind to me which."

"With pleasure." Tom shot once, the bullet hitting dead center in Johnny's forehead.

"Now we better get out of here," Gavin said, "before the security guards show up."

"Damned straight," Tom replied. He saluted Mick while heading to the door. "It's been...interesting. I doubt we'll meet again, though."

"Probably not," Mick agreed.

As soon as Tom was out of sight, Gavin gripped Mick's shoulder and a second later, they had returned to the place where Mick had left the car in the shadows at the backside of a darkened parking lot two blocks from the building.

Chapter Thirteen

"How are you feeling?" Gavin asked with concern as he and Mick packed up their few belongs in preparation for going home.

"Betrayed." Mick sighed. "Probably not as badly as Johnny felt it at the end, but damn it, Gav, how could he let her do that to him?"

"Love, I suppose. Pretty twisted love, but nonetheless that's what it was. At least in his mind."

"Remind me never to fall in love," Mick said morosely. "I'll stick with what we have. Good friendship and good sex."

Gavin nodded, zipping up his bag. "And caring about each other." He smiled softly. "More than we have for anyone else in our lives—in that way at least."

Mick looked at him, returning his smile. "Perhaps you're right. I suppose time will tell if it's for real."

A few minutes later, they were back in the condo. As he unpacked his things, Gavin thought about Mick's words.

He's right, we do have something that's good between us. Love? Maybe. Although I suspect that neither of us has the capacity to love—or do we? Does it matter? Not in the grand scheme of things, I think.

He smiled when Mick came to stand in the doorway to his bedroom. "Come here," Gavin said, holding out his hand.

Without hesitating, Mick came to him.

"I think we need to—well, celebrate might not be the word I want—but..."

Mick nodded. "End what has been a very grim few days with something that makes us feel it wasn't a total loss?"

"That's one way to put it."

Mick's mouth tightened. "I don't think I'll ever... This was worse than that man I told you about."

"The one who you thought you loved who tried to rat you out?"

"I never thought I loved him. But I did trust him. Just like I trusted Johnny." He looked at Gavin, pain in his eyes. "Am I that...needy, that if someone seems to want me in their life...? Seems to want me as their friend, I immediately have to believe that they are being truthful about it and not question that they might be doing that so they can use me?"

"Mick," Gavin replied, taking his hands. "We all need friends. You, me, everyone." He pulled Mick into a loose embrace. "Do you think that's what I'm doing? Using you?"

"I..." Mick shook his head. "No. No, there's something different between us. Maybe it's because of what we've both gone through, but as you said, and I'm beginning to believe you, I think we're more than just friends in the general sense of the word. It's not love," he said, echoing Gavin's thoughts, "but it's deeper than just two men working together and living together because we're...compatible?"

"Compatible, yes, and more. We understand each other, so maybe it's the beginning of love?" Gavin chuckled softly. "We get that our moral code is sadly lacking as far as most people would be concerned but for us that's just how it is."

Mick nodded. "Us against the rest of the world and damn them all."

"Exactly. As you once said, if we didn't do what we do, someone else would. We might as well make a profit off of people whose morals are no better than ours." He released Mick then, pressing his hand against Mick's groin. "Just in case you didn't get it, all this talk is not why I called you in here."

Mick laughed. "You didn't call me in, I came in. And I was obviously having the same kind of thoughts, so..." He stepped back. "Strip. Now."

"Yes, Sir," Gavin replied, lowering his gaze as he pulled off his shirt, his cock instantly hardening painfully with his thought of what would happen next.

* * * *

"I found us a handler," Mick said a week after they had returned from Chicago.

"Someone you trust?" Gavin asked, leaning over Mick's shoulder to look at the very carefully worded email.

"As much as I trust anyone in this business, I guess, given what happened with Johnny." He smiled dryly. "At least this person is married and her husband works with her as one of her hit men."

"How many does she have?" Gavin wanted to know, not blinking an eye at the fact that it was a woman.

"Three, according to the person who recommended her."

"And that would be?"

"Someone I worked with before I hooked up with Johnny. Dishonest as the day is long but he has no reason to steer me wrong."

"Well, if you trust him, I guess I do too. So tell her we're in, as a team."

"Will do." Mick typed a very short, very innocuous email, hit send then they waited. Twenty minutes later, via Mick's heavily encrypted second account, they got a reply from an equally encrypted account belonging to the woman.

"She has a job for us. A test case, as she puts it. We do it successfully and she'll take us on."

"Then we'd better get our butts in gear."

Mick laughed. "We'll do that after we finish the job."

"Smart ass," Gavin muttered.

"Always, these days," Mick agreed. He replied to her email, sent it off and moments later got one back with the details of the hit.

From there, Gavin was glad to discover, it was life as it had become for them. He and Mick successfully completed the job and soon were kept busy with others.

And between jobs. Gavin looked at Mick and smiled. *We spend our time doing what two men who care about each other do.* He pocketed the airline tickets he was holding. *Traveling some, screwing a lot, and generally enjoying the life we've made for ourselves. Things are getting better.* He nodded. *And for damned sure they could have gotten worse, if we'd let them. I guess that's what...caring for someone does. Makes life, if not perfect, at least worth living. Who knows? Maybe someday we'll get up the courage to believe love is possible, even between two men such as us. Until then, live like there's no tomorrow, cliché as that is, because considering what we do...* He shelved that thought instantly.

"Get your ass in gear," he said to Mick. "We have a plane to catch."

About the Author

Born and bred Cleveland, I earned a degree in technical theater, later switched to costuming and headed to NYC. Finally seeing the futility of trying to become rich and famous in the Big Apple, I joined VISTA (Volunteers in Service to America), ending up in Chicago for three years. Then it was on to Denver where I put down roots and worked as a costume designer until just recently.

I began writing a few years ago after joining an online fanfic group. Two friends and I then started a group for writers where they may post any story they wish no matter the genre or content. Since then, for the last three years, I've been writing for publication. Most, but not all, of my work is m/m, either mildly erotic or purely 'romantic', and more often than not it involves a mystery or covert operations.

Edward Kendrick loves to hear from readers. You can find his contact information, website details and author profile page at http://www.totallybound.com.

Totally Bound Publishing